...or Mike McCor...

"Gives Ian McEwan and Edgar Allan Poe a run for their money . . . Decay and ruin seep through this book, drive by some of the finest prose to have emerged in over a decade. The Irish short story is thriving, and in the hands of writers like McCormack it can only continue to."

—*London Independent*

"In the sixteen short stories that make up his first book, McCormack displays the satiric sense, religious knowledge, dark humour, cutting insights and incredible imagination that made Swift famous. Then McCormack adds an overcast of modern doom and gloom with the skill of Edgar Allan Poe. The result is stunning and irresistible."—*USA Today*

"I am a huge admirer of Mike McCormack's work. From sentence to story the writing is by times intriguing, funny, surprising, disturbing and profound."—Lynn Freed, author of *The Servants' Quarters*

"McCormack's language is lovely, lyrical . . . his humor is dark, macabre; the words glimmer like a spell."—*Time Out*

"A cross between *1984* and *The X-Files* . . . *Notes from a Coma* establishes McCormack as one of the most original and important voices in contemporary Irish fiction."—*Irish Times*

"A major talent in Irish fiction . . . McCormack slyly and brilliantly satirizes, among many other things, our fixations with celebrity and high-priced medical technology."—*Booklist*

"McCormack is the most exciting new writer to emerge since Pat McCabe."—*Irish Book Review*

"McCormack's debut crackles with wit, is laced with black insight and places him right up there with McCabe as a master of the new Irish Gothic."—*Sunday Tribune*

"Irish writer McCormack's debut collection (he is winner of the Rooney Prize) is a dark meditation on life and death and the states of existence that fall somewhere in between . . . The pages are populated with ax murderers, self-mutilating artists, stalkers, and pre-teens who give us step-by-step instructions in building pipe bombs but also fathers and sons, brothers and sisters, and troubled young men torn between love and hate. And underlying the macabre plots is a sense of humanity and subtle humor."

—*Library Journal*

"Comparisons to Poe are apt . . . there's no denying McCormacks knack for throwing a harsh light on some of life's grimmer corners. Disturbing, audacious work."—*Kirkus*

FORENSIC SONGS

FORENSIC SONGS

Mike McCormack

First published 2012 by The Lilliput Press, Dublin 7, Ireland
Copyright © 2012, 2014 by Mike McCormack

Published in 2014 by
Soho Press, Inc.
853 Broadway
New York, NY 10003
All rights reserved.

The author would like to thank The Arts Council of Ireland, An Chomhairle Ealaíon, and the Civitella Ranieri Foundation for their support.

Published by
Soho Press, Inc.
853 Broadway
New York, NY 10003

Library of Congress Cataloging-in-Publication Data
McCormack, Mike, 1965–
Forensic songs / Mike McCormack.
     p. cm
ISBN 978-1-61695-414-7
eISBN 978-1-61695-415-4
1. Interpersonal relations—Fiction. 2. Self-perception—Fiction.
3. Ireland—Fiction. I. Title.
PR6063.C363F67 2014
823'.914—dc23   2014006293

Printed in the United States of America
10 9 8 7 6 5 4 3 2 1

Contents

The Last Thing We Need // 1

The Great Lad // 17

Beyond // 35

The Man from God Knows Where // 43

There Is a Game Out There // 61

There Are Things We Know // 89

These Two Men // 107

From the City of Dolls // 119

Of One Mind // 125

Heaven's Mandate // 143

Forensic Songs // 151

Prophet X // 181

FORENSIC SONGS

The Last
Thing We Need

Using the edge of his hand, the sergeant swept to one side the little bits and pieces that littered the top of his desk—a spool of thread, a little coil of silver wire, a neat little pliers and what looked at first glance like a small mound of hair and feathers. With a large space cleared in the centre of the desk, he laid down a sheet of blotting paper and placed an unusually hairy-looking insect in its centre. Only then, stark against the white background, was the hook concealed within the coloured hair and feathers visible.

"The Olive Gold Invicta," the sergeant announced happily. "What think ye of it?"

The question fell to the young guard who stood on the other side of the desk. He looked nervous, giving the giddy impression that he might bolt from the room at any moment. After a long pause and with the cautious tone of a man taking a considerable gamble he said, "It's lovely."

The sergeant smiled indulgently. "It's more than lovely, young fella, it's downright irresistible." He turned the fly over so that now it presented an iridescent green belly to the light. "You're not looking at it properly. If you were a brown trout, about two and a half to three pounds, say, and this lad lit on the surface over your head, you'd be beside yourself with happiness. One lep out of you and you'd have him." He looked up brightly. "Of course then I'd have you and that's when we'd have some sport."

And for a few moments the sergeant was lost in such a happy, heedless reverie that the young guard thought it best to remain silent. When he came back to the present the sergeant's tone was fond. "I started tying flies shortly after I came here—learned it from a man by the name of Billy Phelan. You wouldn't know him—he's dead now this good while. Billy would come into town every Tuesday to draw his pension. He'd buy two plugs of tobacco and that would do him till after second Mass on Sunday. But he'd break your heart, the same Billy. Trying to get him into a hackney at night to take him out home ... many's the night he slept in one of the cells. But for all his faults there was no one to tie flies like him." And with that the sergeant sat back and looked up at the young guard. "So tell me, what do you have?"

Startled by the sudden change of subject, the young guard's head jerked from side to side. "Nothing," he blurted, "not a thing."

The sergeant squinted at him. "There can't be nothing, there has to be something."

The young guard looked down at the fly on the desk and repeated, "There's nothing, we've looked everywhere."

"There must be something, some few pages, a document of some sort or other."

The young guard swallowed thickly.

"There must be some sort of a sketchy outline or a synopsis of some sort."

The young guard remained silent. The sergeant leaned forward onto the desk.

"What about all the obvious stuff—a short account of his inability to get on with a silent and sullen father?"

"None whatsoever."

"No tender account of loving regard for his sainted mother?"

"No."

"A disturbing account of clerical abuse?"

The young guard shook his head, his misery now deepening as the note of incredulity thickened in the sergeant's voice.

"We hadn't much but what we had was clean—something along those lines?"

"No."

"Any description of him wearing a sleeveless *geansaí* or of his head hopping with lice?"

"No."

"Short trousers?"

"No."

"No account of him going shoeless through the fields and developing a thick, protective callus on the soles of his feet?"

"No."

"A harrowing account of his struggle with the *Modh Coinníollach*?"

"No."

"Any character sketch of him looking up with fright and bemusement at the adult world, an account possibly offset in the third person?"

"No."

The sergeant considered a moment. His face was furrowed with anxiety. "A small parish publication, it'd be easy to miss?" he ventured quietly.

"None."

"A vanity publication, badly edited on poor-quality paper, loads of typos?"

"No."

"No sign of a tattered manuscript anywhere? Possibly in a small box that might have fallen down the back of the dresser?"

"Nothing, we did a full search, the house and outhouses, all clean."

"The fridge, did you check the icebox?"

"A block of ice cream, nothing else."

"Suffering Christ," the sergeant breathed, visibly awed and beyond caring who saw it. "And how did he account for himself?"

"He shrugged his shoulders."

"He shrugged his shoulders?"

"He shrugged his shoulders and produced a birth certificate from a coarse bag under the bed; that's all."

The sergeant finally snapped and surged to his feet. He threw his hands wide. "Fuck the birth certificate," he roared, "where's his ISBN?"

Had he taken the moment to look, he would have seen that the young guard was trembling on the verge of tears.

"It's no one's fault," the sergeant amended an hour later, his fit of temper behind him. "He might be one of those anomalies the system throws up from time to time. He might be, but I doubt it. I have a feeling . . . Either way, the thing is, what are we going to do about it? Tell me again what we know about him."

The young guard turned a page of his notebook hurriedly, relieved to finally contribute something positive. "We have his name, date of birth, educational records, and invoices from his place of work."

"Which is?"

"He owns a small breaker's yard beyond the quarry, a busy spot; he employs two other men. We also have several bank statements and electricity bills. He has a wife and two grown-up sons, all of them fully compliant; they were severely embarrassed."

The sergeant snorted dismissively. "None of that's worth a damn. How did he justify himself?"

"He said it slipped his mind."

"Slipped his mind! How the hell . . . you'd swear to Jesus we were talking about a dog licence."

The sergeant opened a drawer and pulled out a glass and a small bottle. Ignoring the young guard, he poured himself a generous measure and drank. He looked off into the distance, his gaze lost in the white walls of the barracks. Then, turning the glass in his hand, he asked the young guard, "How long are you here now—two, three months?"

"This is my eighth week," the young guard said, wanly.

"Eight weeks," the sergeant sighed, "and this is what you come up with—the only man in this jurisdiction not to have written a childhood memoir." He pursed his lips and shook his head in disbelief. "That's some start to a career in law enforcement." He sipped from the glass and thought for a moment; then he motioned to the chair by the wall. "Pull it over and sit down. I'm going to tell you something."

The young guard swung in the chair, embarrassing himself again by clattering it awkwardly off the front of the desk. When he was seated the sergeant began by sweeping his hand across the room.

"I come in here every morning and I sit at this desk and the first thing I do is study all overnight intelligence and activity. I analyse and interpret and then I collate my conclusions with the Threat Matrix for this jurisdiction, chapter and verse, all twenty-seven pages of it. Then, in light of my analysis, I reprioritize anything that needs reprioritizing and I finish up by submitting my daily report. That done and God in his heaven and all other things being equal, I put the whole lot back in the vault and I open my paper and drink my mug of tea. I've been doing that for nearly forty years and I have never had a security breach like we're looking at here. Now, I'm two months away from retirement, two months away from a civic reception with a lot of nice speeches and a small gold watch with the force's crest inscribed on the back of it. But now . . ." he motioned toward the young guard's notebook, "this lad crops up." He gazed off into the middle distance, a gloomy expression swelling his features. The effort it took to control his frustration made it necessary for him to place both hands on the desk. "Is there anything to be gained by bringing him in for questioning, I wonder?"

"It's standard procedure," the young guard reminded him.

The sergeant nodded. "So it is. Okay, let's bring him in for questioning. Let's get a full account from him, names, dates, a complete timeline. Bring him in."

The young guard turned and left. With the room now empty the sergeant leaned back in his chair and stared up at the ceiling. His tone was ragged with aggravation and fatigue; imploring. "The self as the first object of suspicion—each man responsible for his own surveillance. What, exactly, is so difficult about that?"

Later that evening the young guard's expression was one of open wonderment. In the dim light of the barracks his eyes fairly spar-kled with disbelief.

"One man, one dole form," he breathed, "I never knew you minted that."

Behind his desk the sergeant trimmed away some loose hairs from the end of a golden fly. He spoke without looking up from his work. "You couldn't keep track of them," he said, his face expressionless. "Whatever chance you had in winter when things were quiet, you had none at all in summer when there was work to do. You'd have lads off building bits of houses, and lads cutting silage and other lads off to the bog. One of them would round up all the dole forms in the parish and drop them in here. I had to put a stop to it, I didn't know down from Adam who was coming or going. It got so bad I couldn't put a face to half the names coming across the desk to me. I couldn't tell whether there were hundreds of men out there on the dole or whether there were only a handful of men drawing benefits for hundreds of spouses and dependents. I had to put a stop to it."

"I answered a question on it in my final exam," the young guard said happily. "'*Voluntary compliance has its roots in the doctrine of one man, one dole form. Discuss.*' It's still part of the core curriculum."

The sergeant smiled. "I was asked up to the college to give a lecture on it but I got out of it some way or other. There are better men than me standing in front of an audience speechifying. How did you score on it?"

"I got a B plus."

"You were happy enough with it?"

"Yes."

"Good."

The sergeant blew twice on the fly and held it up to the light. Satisfied, he laid it to one side of the desk and drew a thin sheaf of papers toward him. He eyed the documents with distaste. "So, this gent below, what did he give us?"

"Twenty-two pages, about seven thousand words."

"Give me the gist of it."

"It's the usual story. A poor upbringing at the heart of a large family dominated by an unsympathetic father; a saintly mother who intervenes from time to time on his behalf but who is largely left drifting around to no effect in the background. There is a poignant account of sharing a small truckle bed head to toe with two brothers and two sisters. It's the standard telling."

"In summary."

"In summary, a plucky and ultimately forgiving story of a marginal victory over poverty and adverse parenting." The young guard sat back.

"Nothing subversive?"

"No, nothing we have not heard a million times before."

"And what the hell was so difficult about that," the sergeant wondered aloud. "Are there any internal inconsistencies or contradictions in it? Is he indexed and referenced in the other contemporary accounts?"

"Yes."

"And in all the revised and expanded editions?"

"Yes, several times and they all tally with his version. He flew through the polygraph, as well."

"What did the Profilers say?"

"They concur with his account; they can find nothing in it which points to a pathology of evasion or non-disclosure."

"Nothing political?"

"No."

"Did they give a recommendation?"

"No."

The sergeant snorted scornfully. "I'll bet they didn't, the fuckers; say nothing that might hang them. See what they're doing there, washing their hands of it, disclaiming any responsibility. You want to watch out for that."

The sergeant considered. Evidently, things had come to a crucial juncture. By way of gathering his thoughts he swept some imaginary pieces from the surface of the desk, using a rhythmic sweeping motion as he considered. When he finally spoke it was clear he did not wish to clutter an already complex situation with further possibilities.

"The way I see it, this gent presents three options: firstly, and however unlikely it may seem, it might be an honest omission on his part—he may indeed have forgotten, in which case it means nothing in security terms; that's the first option. The second option is that the omission is intentional, that it is part of a plan and that this man presents a direct if as yet unspecified security threat. Or the third—and this is the worrying one—such an omission and the questions which arise from it may in fact be a decoy, something to draw the eye and resources from wherever it is the real threat is being developed."

The young guard noticed how the sergeant was transformed by his own thoughts. Now there was a sharpness to him, a swiftness of a piece with his sudden reasoning.

"And you showed him the machines?"

"Yes."

"Gave him the full tour?"

"Yes."

"How they worked and the damage they can do?"

"Yes."

"And?"

"It didn't knock a stir out of him."

"No!" The sergeant grimaced and swore. "That's not good. That's the last thing we need, cranking up those machines."

The sergeant pursed his lips and sat looking into space for a long moment. Then he let his gaze drift to the edge of the table. He picked up the fly and turned it over in his hand.

"Hacklers Muddler," he said, "one of Billy's finest. He claimed it was the first he ever tied. The same Billy claimed a lot of things, though; you couldn't believe the Lord's Prayer from him."

He laid the fly on the desk and continued. "There's a great story about Billy, about the time he came up in front of Judge Hanlon . . . Billy got caught red-handed with half a dozen salmon in the boot of the car. The bailiff came upon him one morning on the bank of the river, the boot thrown open and six fine salmon lying in it but no licence. So up he comes in front of Hanlon and whatever was on Hanlon that day he took a liking to Billy. Of course, Billy had no notion of pleading guilty so he starts off some rigmarole about how he was out checking stock that morning and had come upon these salmon lying there on the bank of the river. Then Billy starts playing the part of the upright citizen to the hilt.

'I put them into the boot of the car, your honour, and I was just about to turn them over to the bailiff when he comes along. It was very comical, your honour.'

'You were doing your civic duty as you saw it?' Hanlon prompted.

'Yes, your honour, because there is nothing more abhorrent to me than salmon poaching.'

"I'll always remember that phrase—'nothing more abhorrent.' Hanlon loved the bit of roguery in him and he almost fed him a complete defence that day. But he didn't swallow it whole; he let Billy off with a fine, something like a hundred pound in the court poor box. But it took the full morning spinning out that story between the two of them, Hanlon prompting him along when he got stuck. And if you were to listen to it, you'd think Billy was the most upright citizen who ever pulled on a trouser. I'd have given a lot to have seen him that day in the witness stand with the stick and the hat. There was a big piece in *The Sentinel* about it, two whole pages— there was great reading in it. And you tell me you've never done any fly fishing."

The sergeant shook his head wonderingly.

"You don't know what you're missing. Up there on the river, the sun shining, a flask of tea and a few sandwiches . . ."

"It's skilful work?"

"Oh, it's a lot more than that," he chided. "Time stands still when you're fishing. *God will not subtract from man's allotted span the hours he has spent fishing.* A Babylonian proverb. Those lads knew what they were talking about. They gave us the first calendar and astrology. I'll bet you didn't know that."

The young guard shook his head. "No, I did not know that."

"Well, now you do."

"Yes, I do."

"And you were a teacher, I believe," the young guard said as he stirred two spoons of sugar into his mug of tea. "I read that somewhere."

"I was a teacher for three years," the sergeant said, putting the lid back on his lunchbox and shoving it into the drawer. "The longest three years of my life."

"You weren't happy at it?"

"No, I wouldn't say that. It's not that I wasn't happy at it; it was more that I wasn't suited to it." Now he gazed querulously at the young guard. "You're a man of broad enquiry. I see you there at your desk every day with your head stuck in some book or other. Answer me this. You look at a child and what do you see; a five- or six-year-old, what do you see when you look in their face?"

The young guard shrugged his shoulders and looked down at the floor. He hadn't anticipated a question. He sensed a trap. "A small adult," he ventured carefully, "a solid, compliant citizen in the making."

The sergeant nodded approvingly. "That's what I thought, too, once upon a time. Farmers, firemen, dental hygienists, long-jump invigilators at community games—these are the sort of things you should see in a child's face. But I never saw any of that. I saw something completely different. They'd come in the school gate with their little faces glowing and all I could see were things like . . . *possession with intent to supply . . . conspiracy to defraud . . . public order offences . . . breaking and entering . . . ID theft . . .* awful stuff like that. Plain as day those were the things I saw written across their faces. It took a toll on me. In the middle of my third year I went to the principal and told him about it. He was a kind man but he had no sympathy for me that day.

'Those are the things you see,' he said. 'Well, let me tell you what I see, the things I see before they're even born. I see their parents, young couples out walking hand in hand and all I see between them are things like . . . *mandatory sentencing . . . life plus ten years . . . both sentences running concurrently . . .* if I'm lucky, I might see something like . . . *community sanction.*'

"That startled me I'm telling you, that put me in my place. Imagine living with that, seeing that sort of thing day in, day out. It broke his health in the end, the poor man. He slumped onto his desk one afternoon and was carted off to hospital: a stroke. He lost all feeling down his left side and it was six months before he could walk again. A fine fresh-faced man, he had a daughter doing the Leaving Cert. the same year . . . Anyway, I didn't need twice telling. I threw my hat at it toward the end of that year and joined the force and I wasn't one bit sorry. You wouldn't believe how dangerous children can be. You can't turn your back on them . . ."

They closed the door and stood out into the early night. The sergeant gazed up at the lintel.

"We need to replace that bulb tomorrow or one of us will split ourselves coming out of here some night. That's all we'd need."

They made their way across the gravel toward the sergeant's car. The young guard opened the passenger door and was about to lower himself in when the sergeant placed his flask and lunchbox on the roof and stared across at him.

"Eight weeks you said, that's how long you've been here."

"Yes, eight weeks just gone."

The sergeant considered a moment and then went round the front of the car. He leaned back against the bonnet and folded his arms across his chest and appeared to stare out into the dark night beyond the road for a long moment.

"I'll tell you what we'll do," the sergeant said softly. "We'll release this gent tomorrow morning and we'll put him under twenty-four-hour surveillance—bugs, taps, intercepts, visual, audio, the whole shebang. And when we've done that we'll open a file with his name on it and backdate the first entry to three months ago . . . that's what we'll do tomorrow." He turned to gaze at the young guard who now stood with one foot already in the car. The young guard blanched and stood back from the door. Callow and all as he was, he recognized the deception immediately. His first instinct was to protest. The word was out of his mouth before he could check it.

"But . . ."

"No buts," the sergeant said shortly, "you're young, you don't know the half of it. Take it from me, you don't want to be drawing attention to yourself with something like this. You'll get no thanks for it, mark my words. And I'm only two months away from retirement so I don't want this hanging over me, either. This could go on for years—there will be an investigation, hearings, adjournments, appeals . . ." A thin note of apprehension undercut his speech. "Up and down on that train three or four times a week." He grimaced at the prospect and shook his head ruefully. "No . . ."

And now the young guard truly saw the gamble, what was wagered on it and what its full consequences might well be. And the prospect humbled him. He saw that in backdating the discovery of the anomaly by three months, the sergeant was taking full responsibility for it. And in the event that it turned out to be something more dangerous than an anomaly, the sergeant was gambling on the authorities letting sleeping dogs lie, not seeing the point of persecuting a retired man. And now . . . and now the issue . . . the whole moment was hopelessly blurred—there were too many options, things had been suggested, things proposed, and the young guard was no longer sure what he had agreed to or what he was complicit in. He gulped and raised a hand, then dropped it onto the roof of the car. "But someone like that, he might be capable of anything."

The sergeant nodded. "Yes, he might, and then again he might only be a glitch in the system." The sergeant studied the young guard. The lad had shown genuine acuteness throughout the investigation, a degree of thoroughness and clear reasoning he would not have credited him with. He made a mental note to stress all this in whatever report he might have to write. Also, despite a bookish nature that kept him unusually quiet, the young guard had proved to be easy company in the small barracks. But now the sergeant saw that he really was on the verge of tears and he was embarrassed for him. He could well sympathize. It had been a tough few days, certainly not the sort he would have wished for him at the beginning of his career. He turned and looked out into the gloom.

"How far would you say from here to the other side of the road?"

The young guard bent forward and squinted. The sharp night air had drawn the nervous flush from his face. He straightened up. "About forty yards, give or take a few."

"About that I'd say, forty yards. You know, if you were to leave your cap over there now I'd drop a fly into it from here." And with that, the sergeant stepped away from the car and planted his feet. He drew his forearms back across his chest and with his imaginary rod he cast out over the road. He spoke to himself.

"I mightn't do it the first time, but I'd do it the second."

And he drew his wrists once more behind his right shoulder and cast out again. And as he stood there watching him, the young guard was as certain as he would ever be that he was seeing someone lost in a moment of contentment.

He watched him cast out again into the darkness while above them the sky closed over the earth, a night sky crossed with planes, satellites, unmanned drones . . .

The Great Lad

Christ, he'd always been thin, never a pick on him, but I'd never seen him looking as thin as he was at that moment, standing there in the kitchen with the grey hair hanging in his face and the rain dripping off him like a drowned dog. Not even the old anorak he was wearing could bulk him out to any size. And the little bony hands on him, as well—he'd started rolling a cigarette—I thought I could see all the missing years in the glossy sheen of his hands and the blue veins looping between his knuckles.

And yet, in spite of his appearance, part of me couldn't help but think that he looked well for a man I had thought dead these past seven years.

"You weren't always so short of talk," he said, licking the cigarette and placing it in the corner of his mouth. "Are you not glad to see me, Seaneen? Your older brother? It's not that often I call now, is it?"

He lit his fag, using that awkward stooping motion to bring the fag to the flame instead of the other way around. Small as the gesture was, it opened up a vein of bitter grievance that coursed through me like venom. He's barely inside the door, I thought, and already he's getting to me.

"I thought you were dead," I heard myself say. It was not a good start.

"It's good to see you, too," he snorted, "how long has it been?"

"Seven years," I said.

"Seven years," he repeated wonderingly. "Where do they all go? It only seems like yesterday." He drew hard on the cigarette and thrust the tobacco and matches into the pocket of his anorak. He raised his face and took in the whole of the kitchen and then fixed his gaze on me and there we both stood, wordless and embarrassed and hopelessly at a loss with each other.

"You need to get out of those clothes," I said, "you'll catch your death in them."

He turned his back to me and looked out the kitchen window. A bald patch on the top of his head glistened damp and shiny in the afternoon light. As he turned, the light flowed across his face, hollowing out the lines in his cheeks and along his jaw.

"I'm tired," he said, dipping his forehead into the palm of his left hand and massaging his temples. "It's been a long day; I think I'll have a bit of a lie down." He bent to pick up the suitcase and I saw that it was as much as he could do to lift it. "Is there a bed above in the old house?"

I took the key off the dresser and handed it to him.

"There are blankets in the cupboard," I said as he passed through the door. "I'll call you in a few hours."

"Don't bother, leave it till tomorrow, we'll talk tomorrow."

With his back turned, he raised his hand in a parting salute and left me standing in the silence of the kitchen once more.

A small pool of water glistened on the tiles where he'd stood. Margaret entered from the hall, Jimmy draped over her shoulder.

"I thought I heard voices," she said.

I stared at the little pool of water on the floor. Had I not seen him leave with my own two eyes I might have thought that for the second time in his life, my older brother, Jimmy Cosgrave, had disappeared into thin air.

They were a four-man team at the time, working out of a yard in Edmonton, covering north of the Thames in a Transit van: four men from the same parish, four men who'd grown up together, four men riding out the hard years of the eighties in the land of dope and Tories.

After breakfast in the yard, they'd load up the tools and fill two barrels of diesel; then they'd hop into the van and head out to one of the gippos' campsites in Lewisham or along the A13 near Dagenham. They'd pull in there on the campsite and wait and sure enough, after a few minutes, the green van would draw a crowd. The caravan doors would open and all these gippos would pour out, every one of them big bastards, arms like gorillas but sound enough if you kept the right side of them. One look at the green van and they'd know the craic.

"What part, lads?"

That's how it was with gippos, always had to know who they were dealing with—the price of doing business with them. The lads would leave the talking to Jimmy.

"A small village in the west, you wouldn't know it."

"Tell me the name and I'll know it."

"Louisburgh, south Mayo."

The big gippo nodded. "I know it well, many's a bad roll of lino I sold in it. God's Pocket, am I right?"

"You know them all."

"I'd know less, what have you got?"

The going rate at the time for a barrel of red diesel was thirty pounds. One of the lads would push it out the back of the van with his boot and a crowd of hardy-looking gasúrs would roll it away.

"That's one of Gaughan's vans?"

"Yes."

"Out of Edmonton?"

"The very place."

"Throw the keys under her tonight—there'll be a tonne in it for you."

Jimmy guffawed and climbed into the van. "Will I fuck throw the keys under her tonight. I'll be back for that empty tomorrow. We'll talk again."

"Sound."

When I went up to the old house the following morning he was standing at the kitchen window, looking out across the yard. He motioned into the grey light.

"A lot of changes," he said. "All the old sheds and the hen house gone. What's that you're putting up in the haggart?"

"A slatted house, we should have the roof on in a couple of weeks."

"So the old man left a big lump behind him?"

"The old man left very little behind him. Any penny he left goes to looking after herself. Are you going over to see her?"

He ignored the question, turned his back and leaned into the narrow window, bracing himself on one flattened hand. "What time is it now?" he asked.

"After nine," I said, "half-nine."

"Half-nine," he repeated. He nodded out to where a van had pulled into the bottom of the yard. The doors opened and three men spilled out. Jimmy shook his head.

"This is a strange time of day to be starting a job of work, half-nine."

"Leave them alone, don't go down annoying them."

Jimmy laughed ruefully. "Those lads will break no harness by the look of them. Who are they, anyway, any of them local?"

"They're all local, one of them is your brother-in-law."

A broad look of surprise opened his face. "Which one?"

"Frank Moran."

He shook his head. "That's not telling me much; Morans are ten a penny in these parts, or at least they used to be."

"Frank Moran from Roy."

"One of the Lollies?"

"Yes."

"And they have a sister?"

"Yes, her name is Margaret and she wants you down for dinner this evening."

It took him a moment or two to come to terms with this piece of news. "Sound," he said eventually. "I'll change into my evening wear. I'm looking forward to it."

"Whatever you want. And by the way, there'll be someone else at the table."

"A visitor?"

"Not a visitor, our son, his name is Jimmy."

Thursday morning they'd drive to Archway and get the papers: two copies each of The Mayo News, *the* Western People *and the* Connacht Tribune. *Then, another hour driving round looking for the manhole, Padraic calling out the directions to Sean from the* A–Z.

"Listen to this . . ."

As usual, Jimmy had turned to the courts pages. He always got a great kick out of reading them. "Let's see what the poor people are up to"—*that was his spake every time he opened the papers from home. Settling himself on a pile of overalls, he spread out his legs.*

"Listen to this," he began. "'Man Terrorizes Punters in Public House. Late-night drinkers in the Swan Tavern, Ballinrobe, had a lucky escape when local man Thomas Shevlin entered the public bar at twenty past ten on the night of March 21st with a chainsaw. Witnesses reported the defendant stood in the middle of the bar and fired up the chainsaw and then demanded drink. "I was only trying to get their attention your honour," the defendant said.'"

Jimmy looked up. "Right enough, a two-stroke Husqvarna will get you plenty of attention in a pub."

"What did he get?" Martin asked.

Jimmy shifted his back against the metal panels. "Wait till you hear, this is the best part. 'Justice Hannigan,'"—Jimmy raised his head and grinned over at Martin—"My old buttie, Justice Hannigan, who else? 'Justice Hannigan deferred sentencing pending a psychiatric report. He ordered the defendant bound to the peace and his movements confined to within a two-mile radius of the town's Telecom mast. Leave to travel would only be granted with documented proof of gainful employment.'"

Jimmy closed his eyes and bared his teeth in silent laughter, his shoulders bobbing. "Imagine that, Ballinrobe is now an open-air prison for that man."

"Gainful employment my arse," Padraic scoffed, "that man is rightly fucked."

Finding the manhole, they'd lift the cover and Jimmy would suit up to go down and pour diesel into the penstock. Martin and Sean would cordon off the hole with bollards and caution tape and Padraic would ready the tools in the back of the van. After two years working together they had the job down to a minimum of wordless movement and effort. That done and the van parked up, it was time for the bite of grub. They'd find the nearest

*pub and get the grub and the drink out of the gippos' money and then
settle down for a couple of hours, talking and smoking and reading till
the place cleared and went quiet for the Holy Hour. That was when
Jimmy would phone up the yard. He'd stand at the end of the bar
with the public phone cradled between his neck and shoulder, his boot
tapping the bottom of the wall. Their supervisor at the time was a lad
called Gary Withe, a cockney who didn't know a whole lot about what
they were doing but who left them alone and generally took them at
their word.*

*"I dunno," Jimmy would say in a worried tone, "two barrels of
diesel have gone down but it's not moving. When was it opened last?"*

*Jimmy would stand nodding and then, after a moment, ". . . well,
if it's twenty years ago it's going to be a bastard to move, it'll be rusted
solid. We'll need another few hours for the diesel to cut."*

*Another pause and then, ". . . right so, see you tomorrow, Gary . . .
sound."*

*That phone call had them clocked in for three hours' overtime and
that was when they did their day's work.*

He settled quickly into a routine. He'd get up before eight o'clock
and have a mug of tea at the kitchen table while he listened to the
radio. Then he'd wash and shave and by the time he'd have all that
done I'd have finished my jobs and I'd call in and have another
mug of tea with him and we'd talk about whatever had been on
the news that morning.

He had aged something fierce; seeing him stripped of his old
anorak for the first time startled me. All his sinewy muscle had
wasted to a decrepit middle age that was frightening in a young
man of thirty-five. And there was also a real cautiousness about
all his movements, the way he walked and the laboured way
he folded himself into a chair. Everything about him gave the

impression of someone who had skipped over an essential period of their life and it was now a fact that the two calendar years between us stretched to a generation.

And so far he had said nothing of the last seven years; shed no light whatsoever on how he had spent them or how they had passed. I asked him straight out but he waved his hand as if dismissing some piece of nonsense, giving me the impression that his past really was in the past and would remain there. So, whether those years had passed in sickness or in drink, in den or in dosshouse, I could not say. All I knew was that there was about him the ragged look of the prodigal who had savagely committed to his fate. I had an image of him during those years walking some London street with the fag cupped in the hand behind his back, walking with that high-stepping stride of his, the walk of a man whose feet had never lost the memory of wet land under them.

But he was as wilful as ever. He ignored completely my warning about going down and annoying the builders. Every morning he'd pull on the old anorak and tuck the bottoms of his trousers into his socks and make his way carefully down by the wall to the bottom of the yard. Once there he'd spend his time walking around the site with his hands clasped behind his back, patrolling like he owned the place. A couple of days after he began doing this, Frank Moran came up and had a word with me; Frank was fit to be tied.

"Don't let that fucker down near us again, Sean. If he comes round our work once more, one of us will swing for him; laying down the law and shaking his head and telling us we wouldn't get away with this or that in England. Keep him to fuck away from us or I'll pack up my tools and go." I passed on this message to him that evening; of course he had a different slant on things.

"Those lads are pulling the piss, Seaneen, take it from me. You're wasting your time with those lads."

I wasn't going to argue with him. Just being around him now made me tired. Every word between us seemed to open up resentments and annoyances that were hollowing me out bit by bit.

"Just stay the hell away from them; they'll be gone in a couple of weeks. By the way, Margaret is going over to see mam this evening, do you want to go?"

It startled me to see how deeply the question flummoxed him. I would not have thought he could be so easily rattled. He shook his head and snorted and turned away in a bluster of confusion. "Better leave her as she is. Sure that woman wouldn't recognize me."

"Maybe, maybe not."

He gazed down at the table and now there was something etched deeper in his face than his thirty-five years. "You're not telling me that in seven years she's improved?"

"No."

"Still singing little songs and 'Adeste Fideles'?"

"It's not always like that, she has lucid spells sometimes and if she mentions anyone it's always you, never anyone else."

I sensed his anger and confusion deepening. I had seen it before, recognized the divided look about him that always had him casting about so savagely within himself. It was a dangerous mood and it usually ended with him lashing out at whoever was nearest, saying something damaging, something you could not walk away from. Time and again I'd seen it, the malignant bastard in him breaking out. And I wanted that now, some savage part of me wanted to meet it head on one final time and have done with it; some part of me that was sure of itself wanted it done with once and for all. But the moment passed and he seemed to wear himself out just standing there, all his vehemence fading through him, tailing off into bitter fatigue.

I pulled my coat from the back of the chair. "Suit yourself; it's what you've always done."

He looked up and his voice was hardened out to a thin emphasis. "That's the last time you'll ask me that."

It was Sean and Jimmy's job to go down and scrape off the rust and grease with cold chisels and lump hammers from around the edge of the door. That done, they'd call up to Martin and Padraic and they'd get the five-foot Stillson out of the van, lock it onto the top of the spindle and lean into it. Twenty-four stone heaving and pulling on the Stillson and Jimmy and Sean down below, tapping the door with two hammers, trying to crack the rust and get it to rise up through the slides on both sides. Once ever they were beaten—on Pond Road in Strafford. After three days, three barrels of diesel and two broken Stillsons, Gary Withe came out to have a look.

"What do you mean it won't open," he said, "it has to open."

"It won't open," Jimmy repeated blandly, tapping the broken wrench handle on the ground.

"How did that happen?"

"Go down you and open it."

Withe stood back and they showed him; Martin and Padraic leaning on the wrench and Sean and Jimmy down in the hole hammering away for ten minutes. No budge. Then Martin went to the back of the van and pulled out an eight-foot scaffolding pole. He slid it down over the handle of the wrench. Jimmy and Sean started climbing out of the manhole—they knew what was coming. Bang! The head of the wrench snapped off and leapt up from the spindle; Padraic and Martin went tumbling over each other onto the street. Withe pulled the handle out of the pipe and examined it.

"Fair enough, close it up, I'll mark it down some way."

And that was their job during those years—a contract from Thames Water that had them maintaining sewer gates and penstocks all over north London. The money was good, there was plenty of overtime and so long as the job got done no one bothered them.

And of course it couldn't last—nor would they have wanted it to. As a temporary circumstance it was ideal but in the long run there was little enough to it, certainly very little on which you could build a life. Not in that country; not, when all was said and done, in that world.

He reached into the middle of the table for the bottle. A late dinner had lingered on over talk and a couple of beers and it was now well past midnight. Margaret had gone to bed, the table was cleared and the dishes were stacked in the sink. It had been a while since I'd sat up so late and the food and drink together were weighing heavy on me. Jimmy, however, always the night hawk, was just getting a second wind. He shoved his feet back under the chair and leaned onto the table to roll a cigarette.

"So tell me, little brother," he said, "how does it feel?"

"How does what feel?"

"This," he said, "all this." He tipped his chin into the light, taking in the whole kitchen. "All this, the wife and child, the house and domesticity and so on. How does it feel?"

"It feels fine, Jimmy, just fine. I'd recommend it to anyone."

He bent to building his cigarette once more. "Would you indeed? I have to say I'm surprised, I would never have figured you for it."

Something in his tone put me on my guard. This might be it, I thought; at long last, the showdown I'd been waiting for. And it didn't surprise me that it was happening like this; Jimmy's timing had always been blunt and sudden. But now that it was happening, I realized that some part of me—some part better left alone—was already rising up inside me to meet it. I pushed my glass into the centre of the table; he took in the move with a wide smirk.

"So it feels good, does it, all this? But what about the books and the big ideas you were into, Seaneen, all the reading you used to do? Did you trade all those big ideas for this—a slatted house and a herd of dry cattle? Hand on your heart, now, was it a fair exchange?" He sat back in the chair and raised his head, puffing a cloud of smoke up into the light over the table. "And I always thought you were going to be the great lad, the lad who was going to go to college and make his mammy and daddy proud." The scorn in his voice drew his lips back from his teeth. There was nothing weak or sour about him now. This was a measured vehemence, something he had obviously nurtured, something he had great patience with. Then, with a savage change of expression, the scorn fell from his face and he squared his narrow shoulders. "I'll tell you one thing, Seaneen, and not two things; you're only a cunt. You always were and always will be. I'll bet you didn't know that."

I spoke as calmly as I could. "No Jimmy, I can't say that I did know that."

He nodded solemnly as if my cluelessness was something he could understand and had anticipated. "It's not something you read in books, right enough. I didn't know it either but it came to me in a flash."

"What's all this anger and bitterness for, Jimmy, what's it all about?"

He stretched out his legs and pushed back. He was all swollen ease and comfort now, settling into himself properly. "This is about you, little brother. The way I see you here now and how that happened." He stretched toward me, putting his face into mine.

"Tell the truth, Seaneen, you were afraid of your shite, weren't you, afraid to go out and have a life of your own, afraid to make any mistakes of your own. You were only ever content to sit back and measure yourself against me, the ne'er-do-well of the family, the one who always made you look good. That's all you were ever good for, amn't I right?"

"That's not how I remember things, Jimmy."

"I'll bet it isn't."

"I remember you being off your head, being stone mad."

Jimmy shook his head. "I was young, Sean," he said evenly, "something you never were."

"You were off your fucking head," I repeated, my voice rising. "You had their hearts broken." I leaned onto the table, ready at last to go toe to toe with him. I'd got a grip on my own rage now, given it focus; this was my house, my table, I wasn't going to listen to this shit. "All those drink-driving offences, breaking and entering and, to top it all, one charge of possession with intent to supply."

"A few fucking plants," he scorned. "For God's sake."

"Bullshit! Mam opening the door that day and a plain-clothes detective shoving a search warrant in her face. I was there; I saw what it did to her."

Jimmy waved a dismissive hand. "A few fucking plants. You'd swear to Jesus I was running a cartel out of the hayshed."

"You might as well have been, how the hell were they to know? The squad car parked in front of the house for a full month, mam and dad ashamed to put their noses outside the door. You broke their hearts."

"That's not how I remember it."

"It's how I remember it. And the killing thing was that you nearly got away with it. You walked away with a suspended sentence. What was it your lawyer said—*He has work set up in England, your honour.* A nod was as good as a wink to that judge."

Jimmy snorted with bitter derision. "That judge was more sympathetic than the ould fella. He met me at the gate that evening and threw the case down in front of me. He told me to turn back the way I'd come, there was a road there that would take me. And then we stood there throwing fucks into each other, hammer and tongs, and the bingo bus came round the turn and every woman in the parish in it, looking out with their mouths open."

"I had to listen to him after that and I never got it clear in my mind which offended him most—what you'd done or the fact that you nearly got away with it."

Jimmy smiled. "I didn't write the law, Sean, much and all as I might have liked to. But those were my sins and my penance; I don't remember your name being mentioned anywhere in that judgment. There was no reason for you to follow me, was there? But of course you had to be the great lad, the man who had to be his brother's keeper, the man who gave up the place in university to go to London on the pick and shovel. Don't go telling me I was the one who broke their hearts because I have a very different memory of all that." His gaze fell to the table and he appeared to slump into a tired, sullen mass. Now his voice came from deep in his chest and it sounded reluctant, sorrowful. "I twigged you after that accident, Sean. I got a proper look at you that day."

"So this is it," I cut across him, "I saved your fucking life and you never forgave me for it. Now I see it."

"No, Sean, you don't see it. But I did, I saw you after that day. I saw the great man in the pub with his little stories, happy as fucking Larry. The elbow on the counter and the ankles crossed, smirking out over the top of your pint like you were doing the world a favour by just drawing breath. I saw then what you'd done—you'd followed me to London so you could be close to the one person in the world who'd make you look good. I saw how you'd passed off your own cowardice as brotherly love. How did you manage that, Sean, how hard did you have to work to sell that lie to yourself?"

"Fuck you, Jimmy, you're going to tell me now that all this is for my own good."

"That's exactly what I'm telling you. I'm your older brother, that's what we do. But first of all I want you to answer me a question. I want you to tell me how does a man go about fooling himself like that."

My hands bunched on the table. Jimmy's eyes lit up. "Forget it, Sean, you were never a fighting man."

"Were you always this pissed off with me?"

"No, I was never pissed off with you. But I never forgave you for pissing yourself away like that." He lay back in the chair and closed his eyes. "I saw you after that accident, Sean, I saw what it really meant and I saw how it was going to continue. You would always be there, always beside me ready to rush in and pick up the pieces when things went wrong. You'd make that your life; you'd content yourself with that. But I couldn't have that on my conscience because I realized that I had dreams for you as well. So the best thing I thought would be for me to go away, to force you to have a life of your own. One day you would come back to the flat and I wouldn't be there. Then you'd be forced to find your own way, make your own decisions, make something of yourself. So that's what I did, I packed a bag and fucked off, left you to your own devices."

A deep groan of anguish broke from me.

"Bullshit, Jimmy! You're a lying bastard."

He raised his right hand. "My hand to God," he said.

"Come down off the fucking cross! You were never cut out for the martyr." My voice rang in the kitchen.

"I'm telling you!"

"Fuck you!"

The door behind me swung open and Margaret stood on the threshold, holding her dressing gown closed at the neck. Her face was white with temper. "You two, Christ! Do you know what time it is? If you want to fight, take it up to the other house. There's a child trying to sleep here . . ."

"This lad," I shouted, surging from my chair, "this bollocks . . ." The chair clattered sideways onto the tiles. ". . . he'd tell you how to live your fucking life, a man who . . ."

Margaret swiped the air with her free hand.

"No, Sean, I don't want to hear it. If it's not one thing it's another. Just take it to hell out of my kitchen."

"I'm not listening to this shit in my own house!"

"I don't want to hear it!"

"The woman is right, Sean, this is no hour; I'm going."

"Damn right you're going." I took a step toward him, stabbing the air in front of his face with my forefinger. "I'm telling you this, Jimmy, if you're bitter and fucked-off, take it away somewhere else. It has nothing to do with me."

He pushed by me into the hall, struggling with his anorak. He pulled open the front door and I watched him duck his head and shoulder his way out into the night.

"It has nothing to do with me," I roared after him into the dark, "nothing to do with me!"

Sooner or later it was bound to happen—an accident biding its time in a set of circumstances, nurtured there from the beginning and then striking out of the blue with no warning; an accident that leaves everything changed and not always in ways that are immediately obvious.

It happened in Finsbury Park, just up the road from where they had the flat in Crouch End. Sean was sitting in the back of the van, pulling on his overalls; Jimmy was already down in the manhole, singing away to himself. Hank Williams, that's what he always sang down in those holes. He reckoned Hank's lonesome tunes carried better underground.

Take these chains from my heart
And set me free
You've grown cold
And no longer care for me.

The singing and hammering stopped and when Sean looked down, Jimmy was sprawled along the concrete lip with his hand to his throat and one foot in the sewer, kicking.

"The rope, Martin," Sean yelled, "Jimmy is down."

Sean shinned down the ladder and hauled Jimmy up into a sitting position. Thin and all as he was, he was still dead weight and nearly unconscious. The details of a weekend safety course came back to Sean in stuttering fragments—don't panic, work quickly and above all don't fucking breathe. He tied the rope under Jimmy's oxters and heaved him to his feet; the lads up top took the strain and began raising him up, Sean clutching him between the shoulder blades, guiding him up the ladder. The manhole was only twenty feet deep but he thought he would never get out of it. Now his throat burned and he was weakening with panic. It was only when Padraic reached in and pulled Jimmy out by the shoulders, it was only then, feeling the fresh air on his face, that he knew he was going to make it. Martin pulled him out and dumped him near the footpath. Beside him he could see that Padraic was already down on one knee over Jimmy with an oxygen bottle and mask. Jimmy's eyes were rolled up into his head and he wasn't moving. Padraic began pumping his chest and yelling at him.

"Come on Jimmy, breathe you fucker, breathe!"

Jimmy suddenly convulsed and jerked over on his side, throwing up in a violent gush. He raised himself up on one elbow and kept puking and then lay down on his back and pulled the oxygen mask onto his face.

"I'm okay," he gasped, "Okay."

Sean would remember this long afterward, how the separate details of these slow moments came together in a blur. Lying there on the side of the road, he was vaguely aware of a small crowd gathering beyond the margins of his vision, peering in at him. Deep within his chest, his heart stumbled and a surge of pins and needles stippled the blood in his limbs. Off to his side, Jimmy had risen up again, for another bout of puking. Eventually the crowd drifted away. Padraic and Martin closed the hole and gathered up the tools.

But the two lads lay there a long time after that, face up to the grey sky, with their chests burning and their eyes streaming.

Beyond

Nathan walks hand in hand with his mother down the stairs of the multi-storey car park. They might have taken the lift but his mother has chosen to come this way, knowing that the stairway, with all its echoes and security decals, will play a lot better to her child's sense of adventure and curiosity. Because this is her mood now: happily indulgent and ready from the moment she decided to keep him from school to give Nathan a day to remember.

They come out of the car park and stand on the pavement while she searches, and draws a pair of sunglasses from her shoulder bag. The sunshine and the throng of people in the street confirm the rightness of her decision; she can do no wrong today.

"I say we get something to eat," she says, "how about that?"

Nathan looks up at his mother. Her eyes are lost behind her sunglasses but he has sensed a kind of giddiness about her all morning. That might not be a bad thing, he feels, because, as far as he can tell, she seems like a lot of fun in this mood. Still though, you can't be sure.

They head off in the direction of Quay Street, to where the restaurants and cafés are. Skirting by the huge building site that is the city park, Nathan's mother marvels that they are still working on it a full two years after they started. For his part Nathan would not have minded stopping for a look—dumpers, bulldozers and cranes are always good for a few minutes' gaze. But there is no stopping his mother, she is into her stride and he needs to work up a little trot to keep abreast of her. Pretty soon they are standing in the middle of Quay Street and she is pointing to a café.

"How about that one?"

Nathan shrugs and takes her hand once more; he has no strong feelings about it one way or another. They head toward the café and to anyone watching there is nothing in their manner of going that would make you fear for them.

Afterward, in an attempt to explain the incident to herself and her friends, she would lower her eyes and with a searching grimace on her broad face say hesitantly, "I don't know, I just stepped into the street and . . ." And with that, her voice would trail off as if words themselves had faltered at this crucial moment. And for a long time afterward—several months, in fact—this was as close as she could get to explaining what had happened. Sometimes she might draw on some small corroborating detail and fix the whole incident against it; something like, "A child came by, she was carrying a small bag." But the following day, in a complete reversal, she would deny both the child and the bag. "There was no child," she would declare adamantly. "At that hour of the morning there was no one in the street but myself." Sometimes, in addition to this she might add, "It was a Tuesday and I was standing at the corner of Augustine and Abbeygate Street." The next day these co-ordinates would have shifted and the whole incident would be situated at the other end of the city on a different day . . . All she knew for certain was that she woke up on the pavement shortly after six o'clock in the morning. Two municipal workers, watering window boxes along the narrow street, came upon her. Her blue security uniform marked her out from those few vagrants who were around at this hour. They turned her into the recovery position and after a moment she opened her eyes and struggled to get up. The workers saw a heavy-shouldered woman in her mid-thirties with hair swept back from a broad, pale face. They sat her up and got her to drink from the open flow of the hosepipe. Later, as they watched her being taken away in a taxi, they would agree that if you were attracted to big women you could do a lot worse.

Her hapless groping toward an explanation tried the patience of her friends.

"It was as if all things existed in that one moment," she would say. "A moment of surpassing plenitude and superabundance, a joyful irruption of all possibility. It was a moment of limitless potential, as if the universe had revisited that instant before its birth, that moment before its limitless potential became lawful and structured. It was a childish moment."

This was the type of gnomic utterance that now dismayed her friends.

Reaching further she might add, "All things existed in that moment, all things and their annihilating opposites at one and the same time and these in their turn negated all down through the galleries of infinity where at its farthest point, it too, in its turn, was negated. It was as if the world indulged in one, sudden flexing of all its possibilities. And it chose to do this in the early hours of the morning when no one would experience it. It was like that," she said, looking imploringly around her, "only completely different. That is as close as I can say."

That said, she would lapse into silence. Her friends would subside in irritation, pursing their lips in anger and disbelief.

Resentment gathered to her.

What was seen at first as an intellectual shortcoming on her part was now suspected to be a wilful hoarding of some sacred knowledge, something to which she did not have exclusive rights.

So they gave her books, both sacred and profane, as the saying goes, so that she might have the broadest parameter within which to speak her experience. These books spoke of the ultimate things, those things of which nothing greater can be thought. She read them and handed them back, shaking her head.

"No," she said, "not even close."

They threw up their hands in bafflement.

"That cannot be," they protested, "these are the uttermost things, the things beyond which it is impossible to speak."

The more irritable among them lost all patience and accused her outright of being perverse, of attention-seeking. She ignored them and went on.

"Nor can it be identified against the things it is not. I cannot say that it was not love, nor that it was not justice. Saying it was not God brings us no nearer the truth, either."

This lapse into antique locutions was the last straw for many of her friends.

She had some idea that maybe her work had disturbed her. One year of night shifts, sitting alone in the control room beneath those security monitors that collapsed the space and time of the shopping mall into four-hour video tapes—had prolonged exposure to this continuous abridgement disturbed the fundamental co-ordinates of her existence? Had something concentric in the recurring emptiness of the shopping mall, the vacant geometry of its car parks and the lifeless façades of the shops and boutiques spiralled down to this moment of collapse? That and the five-year archive of abbreviated time-space that was stacked on the shelves above her head.

After several months' frustrated groping and disappointment in which she found herself drifting thoughtlessly toward the furthest edge of her imagination, she began to come apart—not just within herself but from the world, also. At first it was the simple shedding of the accidental attributes—her shadow and reflection deserted her. And without those echoes of herself there also went an essential aspect of her spatio-temporal co-ordination. All sense of continuance broke down; with no before or after and with each moment stripped of any prior or subsequent reference, all sense of duration atomized.

Nor was there any within or without. Sitting with a friend in a café she found herself bracing her feet to the floor against a giddy feeling of disconnectedness. All relational webs and connections fell away. She was neither beside nor before her friend; she was neither there out of love nor companionship nor gratitude. Gripping the table, she closed her eyes and held her breath.

"Hold onto what?"

Her friend placed a hand on her wrist.

"You were talking to yourself. Hold onto what?"

• • •

Weeks later, in this very same café, she found herself severed completely from all memory and awareness of herself. There was a final and total collapse of all prepositional grammar within and around her. Cast beyond every identity and empathy, she found herself freed into an infinite sense of loneliness. Now she was beyond feelings of sorrow and love and fear. A blunt pressure in her head drew her to her feet. She stood up, uttered a few garbled words, and in the instant before she pitched forward found herself stepping onto an incline that would carry her into a latitude where the fulfilment of those words she could never speak opened up—a latitude beyond this world and possibly and inconceivably beyond God himself.

And at this precise moment, two tables away, six-year-old Nathan is busy with a mug of chocolate and a muffin. His attention is drawn across the room to the pale woman who has risen to her feet and begun to bleed from her nose. He watches as the woman, in a dull reflex, opens her hand and the crimson drops spread in her palm like livid coins. Before she falls, Nathan hears her utter something but cannot say what it is. Then she topples forward across the circular table, landing sharply in the narrow aisle in front of the cash register. Nathan's view of the ensuing commotion is partly obscured by the protective embrace he finds himself swept up in. He struggles to see out over his mother's shoulder, rising above her by planting a foot on the edge of her chair and hauling himself up over her head. He stands there rapt, deaf to his mother's panicked pleas, a querulous expression adding years to his child's face. People congregate around the woman but Nathan has a certain feeling their efforts are futile. His mother has seen enough. With a swift flourish she throws some money on the table and hauls him by the wrist out into the bright sun.

Later that evening he will tell his mother that as he looked out over her shoulder he saw a ghost rise out of the woman's body and that this ghost moved off between the people gathered around her and made for the door without a backward glance. At this point, seeing his mother's face, he will stop. He does not doubt what he has seen but young and all as he is, he knows that adults do not always have eyes for these things. Nevertheless, the ghost lives with him and time after time, down the days and years of his life, he will catch himself keeping an eye out for it. Seven years later he will walk into this same kitchen with a biology textbook in his hand. Pointing to a blue and red diagram of the central nervous system he will say to his mother, "It was something like this. Only made of light. And completely different . . ."

The Man from God Knows Where

Shortly before nine o'clock, Mark Hanlon came out of the service station and headed toward his jeep, which was parked on the farthest edge of the forecourt. It was a fine evening but the September light had declined to a fading glow and any moment now the shutters would come down, leaving the service station in darkness.

He climbed into the jeep and pulled the door shut, then peeled the lid from the cup of tea. He did this a lot lately, mornings and evenings sitting in the jeep with a cup of tea or coffee, watching the station's clientele come and go—the morning tradesmen with their sandwiches and newspapers, the evening customers with cartons of milk and Lotto tickets. Now he settled himself deeper into the leather seat. He liked this jeep, he reflected, everything about it appealed to his recent mood of sullen vehemence. He appreciated its capacity to offend—its bullying contours and greedy consumption—and he would admit also that it satisfied in him some blunt and shapeless desire for revenge.

"A fucking tank," Susan had breathed with disgust when she saw it for the first time. She backed away from it, flicking her wrist as if casting some sort of protective spell against it. In hindsight, Mark recognized this moment as one of many to which he should have been more attentive; there was a lesson there. But right now any remorse he felt on account of the jeep was well outside the armoured space that enclosed him. He adjusted the seat and pushed out his feet.

And he liked these service stations, too. Standing on the edge of towns and villages, Mark always imagined that they held out some large, beckoning promise. It took him a while to get an accurate sense of what exactly this promise was but when it finally came into focus he recognized it as something he had always known. Out here, the myth of space and distance still held to places like these service stations, these staging posts between settlements. While it was always the case that the next village lay less than a couple of miles down the road, it was nevertheless easy to get caught up in a wide vision of rolling countryside within which a man might clear his head and come to his senses—all the different ways in which a man might take the measure of himself.

Those were his thoughts as he watched the shutters coming down and the lights go out. As the forecourt darkened, he drained off the last of his tea, crushed his cup to the floor and turned the key in the ignition.

Lately, whenever he came home after dark, he would kill the headlights at the gate and pull the jeep into the side of the house so as not to wake the old man in the front bedroom. He'd turn off the ignition and wait a few minutes while the engine ticked and cooled: all this as if a too sudden entry into the house might prove a disturbance.

Tonight he marvelled that he had become so mindful of these small considerations. How had that happened? Mark was straight enough with himself to know that considerate was not a word that would spring readily to the mind of anyone who knew him; any man who came home one evening and found his wife gone and a note on the kitchen table telling him so could safely presume himself short of consideration among a whole slew of other things. Even now, six months on, he has a vivid sense of that moment. He saw himself in his working clothes, standing at the table with the note in his hand, his head swimming with concussive waves of disbelief. Barely twenty words long and yet that note had divided the whole world between them—he got space and she got time. As ever, the memory of that moment threatened to swell up and engulf him, so Mark, careful of his willingness to succumb to it, got quickly out of the jeep and walked around the house.

Inside the back door he pulled off his boots and turned into the kitchen. If the old man was still up this was where they would invariably meet, this small back kitchen off the hallway. This was their intersection, the point at which their paths would cross— two ghosts passing on to their separate realms. Sure enough, he was up. He came through the hall in his socks, pushing the shirt into his trousers, smoothing back his hair. Mark watched him pass, cinching his belt tight as he made for the kettle by the sink.

"You'll have a cup," the old man called softly.

"If you're making one."

"I'm making one."

Mark drew a chair from the table and sat down heavily. Outside, at the bottom of the garden, the night had gathered into its full darkness. Beyond the yard light he was aware of the dark bulk of the blackthorn hedge that circled the half-acre site on which the house stood. Over the past two years the hedge had grown tall enough to block off completely any view of the hills to the north. It was one of the things Susan had harped on toward the end. "It's closing around us," she'd protested time and again with that irritable flick of her hand. "Soon we won't be able to see beyond our noses." And it was only when she drew his attention to it that Mark saw how indeed the whole site had become enclosed. How could that have happened without him noticing?

The old man handed him the mug and he raised it to his lips. The scalding heat nearly burned the mouth off him. Why did he always have to make it so hot? The old man smiled, drawing his lips into a kindly grin.

"Tough day?"

"The usual," Mark replied, "were there any calls?"

"No calls," the old man said as he shuffled past, "I'll leave you to it."

Mark sat there a while longer waiting for the tea to cool so he could swallow it in a single gulp. After rinsing the mug under the tap he went down the hall to his bed in the furthest room. He lay on the covers fully clothed and let his fatigue wash through him. His last thought before he fell asleep was to wonder how his life had come to the point where his wife was replaced in his own house by an old man in his seventies, an old man whose presence Mark had become grateful for, but an old man who, in all probability, would be dead in a month. He had considered all this before but tonight these thoughts came with a sharper, nagging insistence.

He weighed and sifted in the darkness and it kept him awake longer than he would have wished.

. . .

The following morning, Saturday, he woke to the sound of someone opening the bedroom door; his father's voice carried loudly over his bed.

"It's no wonder she left, a man too lazy to take off his fucking trousers."

Mark groaned and turned over. He'd lain awkwardly on his shoulder and a vivid pain now lanced down into his forearm.

"The cut of you," his father continued, with the same patient aggression, "it's about time you got sorted out and stopped feeling sorry for yourself: time you stopped acting the bollocks."

Mark sat up and eyed his father straight on. The pain in his shoulder and this sudden ambush had drawn up his temper and now he gave himself over to its full vehemence.

"Acting the bollocks," he repeated slowly, "look who's talking, a man who at my age had already done a six-month stretch in prison, am I right? I'll tell you what we'll do, we'll sit down together this minute and draw up a list of all the stupid things both of us have done up to my age and we'll see who's the bigger bollocks. We'll start with one count of affray and six months at Her Majesty's pleasure. How about that for a start?"

The swollen look on his father's face told Mark he had gone too far. He closed his eyes in dismay and sucked in a deep breath. He couldn't help it; this was how he woke these days, this sudden rising from the depths of sleep into violent moods of black temper, which appalled him for being so savage and fully formed. What the hell was happening in his sleep? Whatever it was, he always woke sore and angry. Now his father raised a placatory hand and moved into the room. Mark was surprised to see him setting aside his ready instinct for further argument; it wasn't like him. This willingness to sidestep a row could only mean that there was something more pressing to hand. Mark braced himself.

"There's no sign of the other lad?" his father said softly.

Mark sighed with relief. "Did you check his room?"

"He's not there."

"He's around somewhere; he might have gone for a walk. Let him be for a while."

His father sat on the end of the bed. The worried look on his face was unmistakeable. "Did you speak to him last night?"

"Just a few words."

"How was he?"

"Fine, same as he ever is."

"He didn't tell you what we did yesterday."

"He didn't say anything, it was late."

His father shook his head and sucked a narrow breath through his teeth. Mark recognized this as a sign that once again the old man had tried his father's patience. The sudden reappearance of his older brother had wrong-footed him in subtle ways. Since his arrival he was less sure of himself, quicker to bluster and lay down the law, quicker to pick hopeless fights for little reason. And right now he looked particularly bewildered.

"The things you find yourself doing," he began. The anxious note in his voice snagged Mark's attention. "I got a call from him around nine o'clock yesterday. Call over, he said, I need to go into town. What do you want to go into town for, I said, I'll bring you the paper. It's not the paper, I've a bit of business. So I call over and he gets in the car and we drive into town and pull up outside the chemist. He does nothing but reaches down into his pocket and pulls up a ball of notes that would choke a horse, all fifties. What are you doing with that, I said, going round with that amount of money on you. He looks at me and tells me that he's going to buy his coffin—just like that, he's going to buy his coffin." Here he paused, giving Mark a moment so that he might credit the incident with some expression of disbelief. Mark shrugged and swung his legs off the bed.

"So he bought a coffin."

"He did but not before we had a big row in the car." He lowered his voice and looked toward the door. "I don't know what put it into my head but I got this idea that he was going to go into Sweeny's and buy a cardboard coffin. For some reason I thought it would be just the sort of thing he'd do to spite us, and it was out of my mouth before I could stop myself. You'll get a right fucking coffin, I said, and not go shaming the whole family in the church. You mightn't have lived right but you'll be buried right. It was out of my mouth before I realized it and of course I regretted it straight away. But that started it—a full half-hour there in the car, the two of us arguing like tinkers. And he gave as good as he got, the fucker, I'll give him that, but he was as pale as a ghost after it and I thought he was going to die there in the seat beside me; he starts coughing and spluttering and then he takes out this bottle of pills and starts wrestling with this child-proof cap, and him still coughing and spluttering . . . I thought he was going to die there beside me . . . and he wouldn't give me the bottle but he couldn't open it and the two of us . . . " His words tailed away in anguish and shame. Mark kept his voice low.

"You should know better than to start arguing with him. You know how much it takes out of him."

"Oh that's easy said, you're gone all day. You don't know what he's like, you don't know the half of it. How did he look last night?"

"The man was out buying his coffin, how do you think he looked?"

Mark stood up and flexed his arm behind his back. He caught sight of himself in the wardrobe mirror and saw a man who looked as if he had been hastily assembled in the dark. His hair stood out from his head and his shirt had lost a button during the night and now hung askew over his bony chest. His trousers were streaked with oil and he cursed inwardly for having handed such an easy opening to his father. He tried hopelessly to smooth his hair down.

"Your mother wants the two of you over for the dinner this evening."

Mark pretended not to hear.

"Are you listening?"

"I heard."

"Well?"

"I'll be there."

"And tidy yourself up, for God's sake; don't come over to your mother looking like that."

"Jesus Christ would you ever . . ." Mark's despairing curse was cut off as his father pulled the door behind him, leaving him standing there in the livid heat of his rage. It took a long moment for him to collect himself but before leaving the room he checked for messages on his mobile; there were none so he tossed it back into the middle of the stale bed.

After he'd showered and put on clean clothes he went into the kitchen. The old man had the table set and was pouring two mugs of tea.

"Get this inside you," he said, taking a plate of chops and peas and fried potatoes from over the range. He placed a small basket of bread in the centre of the table and pointed Mark to the chair.

The smell of food opened up a void in Mark's belly. He hadn't eaten since dinnertime the previous day and the hunger he had gone to sleep on now had him airy and light-headed. He took a piece of bread, squared his elbows and it was a good ten minutes before he spoke.

"The ould fella was here a while ago, he was looking for you."

"I thought as much, I made myself scarce when he pulled up." There was a mischievous glint in the old man's eye and Mark thought that if he was reading his mood correctly it might be safe to probe a little.

"He was saying ye had a row yesterday."

The old man shook his head and smiled. "We had words, that's all. He hasn't changed and neither have I. There was a pair of us in it."

"Like old times?"

"You could say that."

In his blue jeans and T-shirt and with his grey hair slicked back, the old man looked every bit the returned Yank. But his bone-thinness exuded a terrifying and unnatural cleanliness. The insides of his arms glowed pearl-white and Mark wondered if this was one part of his body not running with the filth that was corroding him. This was how Mark pictured it—a black granular filth sluicing through the gates and channels of the old man's body, clogging up the juices and rhythms of his life. And now that he thought about it he was surprised to find that he had no idea where the pancreas was or what exactly it did. Set deep in the soft mass of the belly, he imagined, endlessly sieving and distilling, some task of essential refinement now hopelessly compromised. He picked up his knife and fork once more. "Take no heed of the ould fella," he said, "he's all talk. Are you coming over for the dinner this evening? Mam wants both of us over."

"Sure, why not."

The old man got up to clear the table. This cooking thing was something Mark had not fully got used to. More often than not he would come home at night to find some plate of food ready in the kitchen for him—a bit of stew in a pot or a plate of cold chops in the fridge—nothing fancy but all good stuff and all made with some skill. At that hour of the night there was something tender and unexpected about it, something delicate beyond an old man's desire to make himself useful or pay his way. "It's the least he can do," his father had scoffed when he'd heard about it, "he's getting it all for nothing." Mark did not care for this cynicism. He appreciated the gesture and saw in it the fellowship and consideration of a man who had known hard times himself.

"He ate a good meal," his mother said later that evening, "the heat of the conservatory will put sleep on him." She bent to gather the plates. "Mark, have you had enough?"

"Yes mam, thanks."

"It was nothing; sure you're used to having big feeds now with your new lodger. I'd swear you've put on weight since he's moved in."

She moved toward Mark and placed a kiss on the middle of his head; her milky smell covered him like gauze and caught in his throat. Now that he'd eaten, he desperately wanted to leave. The thought of a few pints before closing time pulled at him, but with the old man asleep it could be a while yet before he got away. His father turned from the fridge and handed him a can. He considered for a moment and then pulled the top from it and drew hard on it; fuck it, why not. His mother stood over him and sighed, her relentless need to comfort getting the better of his wish for silence.

"Don't worry, Mark, this is a good thing you're doing. Offer it up; God will love you for it."

Mark groaned inwardly and found himself repeating an old speech. "The house is there, mam; he can come and go as he pleases and he's no bother to anyone; it suits everyone. You know well he wouldn't have stayed with anyone else."

"Yes but it didn't have to be you, God knows you have enough on your plate," she said, looking pointedly at his father. "He has brothers and sisters."

"Let's not start that at this hour," his father countered sharply from the head of the table. "We've been through this before. That man is in the best place and we all know it."

Before she could open her mouth to reply, Mark silenced his mother with a look; an argument like this could go on all night. He turned to his father. "So has he told you anything yet about the wilderness years? Did he let slip anything when you were rowing with him yesterday?"

"He said damn all, he wasn't giving anything away, still the mystery man, the man from God knows where. You mark my words; that man will talk only when he's good and ready."

Mark had watched his father's baffled frustration deepen over the last three months. Privately he conceded it must be difficult—a brother he had long presumed dead shows up out of the blue with no word of explanation. How do you square that? However he did it, his father had lost surprisingly little time in finding space in the family for the prodigal. After Mark volunteered the room in his house, he had sat with him in this kitchen and listened as he called his brothers and sisters with the news and put them abreast of the new arrangements. A month later he saw him ring them up again, this time with news of the terminal diagnosis. And yet, two months on, his brother appeared to see no good reason why all this effort and kindness on his behalf should be repaid with anything like an explanation or an account of his missing years. He had quietly taken up the room in Mark's house and settled down to the business of dying. When he had time to think about it, Mark found himself torn between an amused admiration at the old man's presumption and a private acknowledgment of his father's frustration.

But since his brother's return, his father had never got a

handle on his own angry confusion. Everything about it had thrown him. Without telling anyone, he had driven up on his own to meet him off the plane at Knock. Hardly believing that he would turn up—that it really could be him after all these years— he had stood alone in the observation lounge with the letter in his pocket that contained word of his coming. Mark had a vision of him standing behind the tempered glass, a shadowed figure peering out over the runway and the bogs beyond. How had such an unlikely vigil panned out like this?

"What I don't understand is how you knew him that day coming across the tarmac. How did you recognize him after all these years?"

"The day at the airport?"

"Yes."

His father considered. "I didn't recognize him," he said carefully, "not the man as such but the cut of him . . . the way he walked and carried his bag, the way he held himself, it all came back to me. I spotted him coming across the tarmac; dressed like a lord he was, the suit on him, the collar and tie, the whole lot. I hadn't expected that—I don't know when was the last time I saw that man wearing a suit."

"You mean you don't remember the last time you saw him at all."

The correction caught his father looking down into his plate. But when he spoke, his voice was soft and certain. "I remember well the last time I saw him; it was outside the billets of the Kerr Addison gold mine in Ontario. That was the spring of 1963, over forty years ago now."

Mark sat up in the chair. "This is the first I've heard of a gold mine. What were you doing in a gold mine?"

"What does anyone do in a gold mine?"

"Mining and . . . ?"

"Yes . . ."

"When?"

"Sixty-two to sixty-three, I said, just the one year. I followed him to Ontario from London in the spring of sixty-two. He had gone over there a year earlier and was making good money and I was in London on the pick and shovel making damn all. So I boarded a boat in Plymouth and docked up in Fairfax two weeks later and got a train overland to Virginiatown in Ontario; I was picked up by the company truck at the station and dumped outside the billets. I spent a year there, digging in the richest gold mine outside of South Africa."

He sat back in his chair, surprised at this lengthy disclosure. He motioned in the direction of the conservatory. "That's where he learned to cook, in that mine. We were grubbing bad in the company canteen—a crowd of Chippewa Indians ran it and they didn't know much about putting on a feed—it was a constant grievance among the workers. But somehow the lad got his hand on a stove and he set it up in our billet. He spliced together a chimney from tin cans and ran it out the window and he would cook away for us in the evening—spuds and steak, the whole lot, he was a great man with the pan. But for him we'd have gone hungry like everyone else. It was no coincidence that we drew down more bonuses than any other crew."

Mark watched his father's attention drift. For a moment he appeared lost in some detail beyond the margins of his tale. When he spoke it was as if he was chiding himself. "You know, if ever I got money that's the one place I'd go back to. Back to those little towns, Kearns and Virginiatown, to see what they're like now, to see what's happened to them."

"I know where I'd go," Mark's mother cut in brightly. "I'd go back to the church we were married in, the church of St. Peter-in-Chains in Stroud Green."

"The church of what?" Mark blurted. From the corner of his eye he saw that his father had now tuned out completely.

"The church of St. Peter-in-Chains. Isn't it a lovely name? It seemed so holy to me when I first heard it, something no one could make up, something straight from God. I knew that when I got married it would be in that church with that name." She smiled wanly and, too late, Mark saw that she'd carved out the opening she'd been seeking all evening. She leaned toward him. "Has Susan been in touch?"

"No," he sighed, "and I don't want to talk about it."

"Be patient," she soothed, "a marriage isn't something you walk away from so easy."

And with that, something in Mark collapsed and he suffered one of his turns. All of a sudden he experienced a heaving sourness toward everything and everyone around him—his mother's scent and his father's presence, this house where he was born and reared, this room and everything in it. He was consumed with disgust toward all these good things, and the worst of it was that this mood was illuminated at its core by a vivid sense of how pitiful he was in these moments, how crabbed and anxious to take offence, to pick fights. And this is what Susan had sensed all those months ago. This is what prompted her to begin the slow withdrawal from him that had ended with that note on the kitchen table. She may not have been able to put a name to these moods but she was smart enough to know that she did not want anything to do with them. And she knew also that they were not something that could be worked through together. This wasn't between them, this was his alone, this was within.

"I'm going," he said quickly, rising from the table. "Wake that man up, he won't thank us for letting him sleep this long. He'll want to wake up in his own bed."

His father saw the look on his face and shook his head in

disgust. His mother squeezed his hand and rose from the table; when she had left the room his father spoke without sympathy.

"I'm telling you one thing and not two things: you need to pull yourself together . . . and fast."

When they got home the old man sat beside the range to pull off his shoes and socks. Mark sat into the table and looked out on the back garden. It came to him that the happiest hours of his marriage were those mornings when he would rise early and sit at this very table with a cup of coffee and watch the day brightening over the fields and the distant hills. He loved those early hours when he could feel the house warming to the new day, the eaves and facia crackling and expanding, the whole structure flexing itself like a living thing in the sun. In such moments he was nearly content and he would sit there until Susan entered the room and saw that look on his face that told her she was never a part of his happiness.

"So he told you about our time in the mines." The old man pushed his feet out and flexed his toes, grimacing with pleasure.

"I thought you were asleep."

"I heard a piece of it."

"It's a good story."

"I'd imagine it is."

"But he didn't say how it ended, why he left; he only stuck it a year. I suppose he threw it all up; that would be just like him."

"No, no," the old man corrected sharply. "It wasn't like that and don't go thinking it was. Your father was as good a man as ever took a shovel into a seam. He was one of the men you send up front to the blast point to shovel out the ore. He was small but he had a pair of shoulders on him and he worked side by side with big Canadians and Norwegians. No, it wasn't the work that

ended it for him, it was something much worse; it was homesick-
ness that got to him. That Christmas we had a few days off so we
sent out for some drink, a crate of beer and a bottle of whiskey
to each man and we sat up on our bunks talking and singing and
telling stories and of course it wasn't long till the crying started;
all these miners sitting around in their bunks, crying for home.
He was young at the time, barely into his twenties and Ontario
wasn't London. I suppose I had a few years on him and I didn't
feel it so hard. Anyway, when he stopped crying he vowed he
would never spend another Christmas away from home. And
he was as good as his word; when his contract was up in the
spring he went back to London and I doubt if he ever did spend
another Christmas away from home."

The old man's voice suited the gloom, it paid out like frayed
rope into the room. Jolted by some new memory, he leaned
forward onto his knees and spread his hands.

"What I remember most—and you can ask him about this
yourself—is going down into the mine at the beginning of a shift.
Seventy-five men standing shoulder to shoulder, naked as the day
we were born and our lunchboxes clasped between our ankles.
Five minutes of a descent in a metal cage, down into the heat and
darkness, five thousand feet. That's what I remember most. Ask
your father, he'll tell you."

"I'm surprised he told me as much as he did; it surprised him
too by the look of him."

The old man straightened up. "That's a miner's thing; mines
leave their mark on a man. They're a melancholy breed, not
enough sunlight. You can spot them anywhere, these quiet men
who stand apart with their heads pulled down into their shoulders, always expecting the worst. I'll bet you see something like
that in your father."

"I suppose so, he's cautious; that's the word I'd use. And that's why I can never understand the six months he did in jail. What was that all about?"

"He's never told you?"

"No, he won't talk about it. I don't even know how I know about it."

The old laughed. "It was nothing at all, just a stupid incident. It happened in one of the dance halls, the Galtee Mór or the Buffalo. A few lads went to battle and as the song goes . . . there were glasses flying and Biddies crying . . ."

". . . and Paddy was going to town."

". . . Paddy *was* going to town, alright. London was a tough station at the time and you didn't have to do much to draw down a custodial sentence in those days. Anyway, your father did his six months and when he got out he headed over to me in Canada. He never told you this?"

"No, he never said."

"Well, don't tell him I told you."

The old man stood up with his shoes in his hand. For a moment he appeared to sway as if caught between two thoughts. "I've a question for you, Mark, a request."

"Yes?"

"When I go I don't want any praying; no prayers, I don't hold with it any more. Can you do that for me?"

Mark smiled and shook his head. "It's a big ask. Dad is regimental, you see that yourself; he does things by the book. And mam's a believer. You'll have to talk to them yourself."

"That's what I thought. But you'll do what you can?"

"I'll talk to them—that's all I can promise."

"Okay."

The old man nodded, satisfied that this last thing was settled. He raised his hand to say goodnight and shuffled from the room.

· · ·

When the end came, it did so with the same faltering stealth that was of a piece with the old man's presence in the house.

His father's car was pulled up in front of the house when he got home that evening. Inside, he heard the unmistakeable murmur of prayer coming through the hall. In the bedroom the old man was lying back on the pillow, his eyes partially open and his upper lip drawn back from his teeth. His narrow breastbone rose and fell like the prow of a small boat. All this was as Mark had anticipated; the old man was a gasper, a man so enfeebled he barely had the strength to die. Mark's mother was down on her knees beside the bed, her hand resting on the hump of the old man's knee. Her head was bowed and she was passing her beads through her fingers.

"The first glorious mystery, Jesus rises from the tomb."

His father stood with his back to the curtains, his hands clasped low on his stomach. Seeing Mark in the doorway, he threw him a defiant glare across the bed. It may have been a challenge, daring Mark to tell him he was doing something wrong here. But it may have been something else entirely. And Mark knew there was nothing generous or forgiving in his own presence at that moment. He moved back into the kitchen and sat at the table where he could hear his mother's voice from the room.

The next few days would be difficult, he could see them clearly. The wake and the funeral, aunts and uncles, people coming and going. His only wish was that the whole thing would be over soon and everyone gone, the house cleared. Then he would have the place to himself once more. He sat listening to his mother's voice coming from the bedroom and when she came to the end of the decade he took out his phone to check for texts and calls.

He was glad to see there was no one looking for him: no one at all, not a soul.

There Is a Game Out There

The last time he walked this landing, Nealon had his wrists cuffed and was facing into the beginning of an eight-year sentence. That was almost two years ago and it was a different age and he was a different man. But right now that's not what's on his mind.

Right now he's wondering why he has been summoned from his cell in the middle of the night.

If the guard accompanying him knows why, he isn't telling him. Less than two minutes ago Nealon had been rousted from his bunk by a voice calling his name in a low bark—Come on Nealon, get up! All he could see from his bunk was the guard's silhouette in the doorway, backlit from the landing. Now, walking two paces behind him, the guard directs Nealon down the landing while all the time whistling a continuous looping melody through his front teeth.

Who the hell goes about their work whistling at this time of night, Nealon wonders.

The guard steers him off the landing and into a lighted cell; he enters behind Nealon but leaves the door open.

The cell is square and windowless, about six metres along each wall and lit overhead by a single strip of fluorescent light; two cells knocked into one, Nealon calculates. Set against one wall is a metal-frame bunk with a mattress, a pillow and a blanket folded on its end: in the middle of the room two metal tube chairs are pushed into a square, formica-topped table. These pieces have a stable, rooted aura about them, as if they have been waiting here in silence a long time. The same cannot be said for what draws Nealon's attention to the corner of the cell—a bulky television set connected to a video-game console with a wireless controller and headset lying on the ground: beside it a large bottle of water with a small stack of clear plastic cups. In spite of the hour and his sleep-sodden mind, Nealon senses a disparity between the appliances, a disjunction of some sort. It takes him a long moment before he solves it; the game console is the most recent model but the television is a deep, lumpish contraption, a dinosaur from the dying days of tube technology. The two technologies have been yoked together across generations in a forced marriage, which is resourceful but which gives the whole set-up a shabby, provisional look.

The guard has thrown himself onto the bed and pulled the blanket up to his chest. He continues whistling absently and Nealon realizes for the first time that this is someone he does not recognize. Two years in this prison and here is a face he cannot place. It would have been hard to miss him, Nealon marvels; the guard is huge, a good hand's breadth over six feet and weighing probably close to twenty stone. He is now comfortably stretched out on the bunk, his bulk sunk into the soft mattress and his head settled into the deep declivity between his shoulders. With a rush of sour feeling, Nealon realizes he has taken an instant dislike to him. Something crude in him cannot resist the idea that this overfed man is marbled through with that vicious streak he has always suspected fat men prone to—their way of getting back at the world, their prissy, sullen point-scoring. It is not an original idea and Nealon is alarmed to have succumbed to it so easily. He knows enough to be wary of first impressions.

"So why am I here?"

The sound of his own voice with its gormless question takes him completely by surprise. It has blurted from him of its own volition and in the brightly lit cell it sounds absurdly comic. Three hours' sleep does not excuse it. The guard's face opens with a thin smirk.

"Why?" he asks with mock concern, "had you plans; were you going somewhere?" He closes his eyes in silent mirth, grinning gleefully, overtaken with regard for what is the dreariest witticism in the prison community. Nealon watches as he drives his humour on with a rhythmic swinging of his beefy leg over the side of the bed. His antipathy might not be so misplaced after all.

Nealon goes to the table and sits down; he needs to concentrate and not lose his focus in such small details. This is the twelfth of September. As far as he can tell, this date holds no personal or institutional significance; there is nothing about it that sets it apart from any other day in the routine of prison life. True, the date lies close enough to the second anniversary of his conviction but not so exactly close as to warrant this summons in the middle of the night. If there is anything Nealon knows about prison life, it is that it moves to its own accurate cycles, its own precisions. Things happen when they should and if this is happening now then this is the time for it.

He turns the date around in his mind, considers it from every possible angle but can find no significance in it.

As for the world outside the prison—all he knows is that today his wife is taking Cuan, their eight-year-old son, to an appointment with the orthodontist. In an unhappy throwback to Nealon's own childhood, Cuan has developed a mouth overcrowded with incisors, a congestion that has thrown his bite out of alignment and that already, at this early age, promises all sorts of neck and spinal discomfort later in life. Today's appointment will decide between the options of a correctional brace or a series of extractions that will be painful but surer in the long run. The whole thing baffles Nealon. Not so much the teeth themselves, whose crooked push through his child's face he has watched ruefully over the last two years, but the pathology inferred from them—the certainty with which something like a child's teeth allows anyone to pronounce the future.

How sure can anyone be about these things, he wonders; how can the future be read from a child's mouth?

There's been a sudden lapse in the flow of time, a fissure into which a whole stretch of it has heedlessly dropped. Nothing else can account for the sudden, vivid presence of the woman who now sits across the table from Nealon. How he missed her entry he does not know; this is something he will have to consider later. But here she undeniably is, already seated and unbuttoning her jacket. She has drawn into the cell a miasmic fur of chill night air and Nealon senses that the temperature around her must be a full two degrees lower than the rest of the cell. With her jacket finally open she draws from it a clear CD jewel case and places it on the table; she looks at Nealon blankly.

"This is what's going to happen," she says without greeting. "This is a video game, Mr. Nealon, and my request is that you play it through and critique it for me—two thousand words should suffice." She taps the case with the tip of her finger and Nealon senses the gesture is timed to signify that the introductory stage of the meeting is now over. He lets several beats fall before he speaks.

"Have we met?"

"No, Mr. Nealon, we have not met."

"I thought so. I'd have remembered if we had, I'm good with faces."

"I know you are, Mr. Nealon, I've read your file."

"Because if we are going to have this dance"—Nealon taps the CD—"I would like to know who I'm taking the floor with."

"My name is Olwyn Crayn."

"Pleased to meet you, now who the fuck is Olwyn Crayn?"

Nealon's deliberate aggression does not faze her. "I'm a consultant. People—businesses and corporations, mainly—come to me when they encounter certain problems or when they lack certain expertise. I consider the problem, research it in so far as I can and then I go out and find someone to solve it."

"A headhunter?"

"I prefer the term human resources."

"You would. So you've considered and researched and come here in the middle of the night to milk my brains."

"As I've said, I've read your file."

Nealon senses that her indulgence is at an end. Evidently she has factored this short bout of fencing into this early part of their meeting but now it has apparently run its course and she is ready to move on. Sure enough she picks up the CD and continues.

"The inlay hasn't gone to print yet so you're going to need some background knowledge, some broad strokes."

"Things will become clearer?"

"Yes."

"I'd welcome that."

"I'd imagine you would." Her voice is a dusty monotone

but for the first time something like a smile crosses her face, a fleeting, vestigial trace of some deep but determinedly hidden impulse.

"Trust me, Mr. Nealon." She holds up the CD and turns it slowly through a full rotation. "This is a video game, a complex, turn-based strategy game. The background scenario is a war zone, an occupied territory at the centre of which lies a prison. The game hinges on a set of demands posted by a cadre of inmates in this prison—their demands are for special category status, the right to wear their own clothes, free association with fellow prisoners and so on. The authorities, for one reason or another, refuse to meet these demands—their reasons are among the things that clarify as the game progresses. Their initial refusal opens the game and you make your first move; you attempt to force their hand by putting two of your prisoners on hunger strike—and so begins the game. From then on, winning becomes a complex, balanced calculus of gaining as many demands as you can while keeping your prisoners alive. At the same time you try to gain enough political capital to enable the prisoners further their cause in the meta-realm of constitutional politics which is outside the prison complex and above the military conflict. You bargain with ten lives, that's your quota."

Nealon's reaction is genuine; his laughter builds to a long, hacking guffaw that drives him back in his chair, his shoulders rocking. "Where do they get those stories from?" he chokes.

"I agree, you couldn't make it up. Mr. Nealon, I've chosen you because of your past and also because you have racked up the hours. Your two years here have been split between *National Geographic* and your game console: two years and you have a whole back catalogue of strategic games exhausted—that's impressive."

Nealon shakes his head. "It might be impressive but it means fuck all. And this . . ." he taps the CD, ". . . you expect me to believe that I'm hauled from my cell in the middle of the night to play a video game, to critique it—I don't buy that."

She nods. "Yes, it does appear trivial and it does appear as if you're being asked to double up on the work of the in-house testers. Because you're right—this game has been played to destruction, all the bugs and glitches have been ironed out and it flows smoothly and without logical contradictions. None of that will concern you, your task is different."

"How different?"

"Let me put it this way. Your task is exactly what the in-house testers cannot do. You have been chosen because of your background, you bring a special sensitivity to the game, a specific mindset."

"A special sensitivity—that's a new way of putting it. And since when did Sony start contracting out critiques to prisoners?"

She shakes her head; evidently he has missed an obvious point. Nealon scrambles to identify it.

"Consider for a moment, Mr. Nealon. Who do you think holds the copyright to this game?"

"Who the fuck cares," he blurts irritably, "some fucking Sony subsidiary, how do I know?"

She gives him time to dwell on his reply, time enough for him to read her stillness as a dismissal of his answer, a silent injunction that he should think deeper, reckon with other, more improbable options. Moments pass and Nealon becomes aware of a pulse building in the side of his head. One thing he is now certain of—she has done this before. No one is born with this kind of timing. Her keen sense of that uncertain instant, which allows her to close in on her adversary—these skills are hard-won and Nealon himself has a professional appreciation of them.

"I'll give you a hint," she continues. "This game is copyrighted to a new, independent, third-party studio with serious financial backing. Want to guess again?"

"No."

"The author's name?"

Nealon shakes his head.

"The principal game architect?"

It takes several moments but when he finally sees it he recognizes also how she has steered him toward it. He speaks very cautiously.

"You're telling me that the author has asserted his moral right."

"Yes."

"The transcendental first cause?"

Olwyn Crayn smiles. "I've never heard that one but yes, if you want to call him that."

"The prime mover?"

"You're getting closer."

"Maigster Ludi himself?"

"Yes."

"P. O'Neill?"

"The one and only."

Nealon's tone is one of pure wonderment. "You wouldn't know whether to laugh or to cry."

"The choice is yours, Mr. Nealon."

"It might be but it still doesn't clarify what it is I'm supposed to do."

"Okay, once you've begun the game you will recognize how the various moves make it progress; it's turn-based, wholly intuitive. Your task is to evaluate the game against sensitivities outside those of a normal beta test. Your response will be a human one."

"Is there any other sort?"

She ignores the taunt. "Your critique has nothing to do with picking out bugs and glitches. I'm asking you to assess how successfully the game engages your sympathies and on which side of the dispute those sympathies lie—with the prisoners or with the authorities. One of the things you will notice is that there has been an honest attempt to depict both sides sympathetically. You will assess how the game's historical sources affect the player's choices. You will assess to what degree a player's prior moral or political convictions affect or inflect his game play. Do the historical sources affect in any way the willingness of the player to sacrifice his avatars? You will notice also that a lot of work has gone into the game's separate environments. Specifically the prison environment; it is a very accurate rendering of the Maze. You will judge how this architecture contributes to the game's feel and atmosphere. How coercive is it, what moods does it provoke in the player—awe, terror, or a reckless wish to destruct? Is the game successful in nurturing a player's sense of responsibility toward his avatars? All these questions, Mr. Nealon."

"More soul," Nealon affirms quietly, "the thinking gamer's cry since the turn of the millennium, *give us more soul.* And this is the gaming industry's response—licensing real-world events?"

"Yes."

"Copyrighting history?"

"It's part of the broader response. This isn't the first time the gaming industry has licensed a real-world conflict but it is the first time it has marketed a conflict as something other than a series of combat missions or stealth attacks. This game confines itself exclusively to the more abstract realm of politics. But you know this story, you've only to look at yourself. The first generation of gamers are now in middle age and they want to move on from strafing aliens and clubbing zombies to something more complex. They're asking for something beyond the racking up of numerical scores, the facile thrill of solving static block and lever puzzles. They want an immersive experience that plays to higher, more abstract values. This game is an attempt to meet that challenge."

"I know the challenge," Nealon replies, "but I will be surprised if this particular game is the answer to it. But now I'm thinking of something else." He pauses to adjust his tone. "So far I'm hearing a lot about your needs but nothing about mine. What's in it for me? You're convinced of my gifts so you don't expect me to work for nothing."

"You mean payment?"

"Of course, let's not be shy."

"I have considered it."

"You have?"

"Yes, very carefully."

"And."

"And I'm thinking of something that is more of a reward than a payment."

"Call it what you like."

"You get to make a speech."

"What sort of speech, a moving plea?"

"No."

"An appeal for calm?"

"No, something more complex; you get to make a case for yourself."

Nealon throws up his hands in disgust. "I tried that, I met a tough audience, twelve good men and true, they were unsympathetic." Nealon is surprised at the depth of bitterness in his tone.

"Yes, I read the trial transcript, I didn't buy it either. Mr. Nealon, I don't have to remind you that your wife has opened divorce proceedings and that her terms are likely to be severe. We both know that she is going to seek sole custody of your only child; she has already sworn a twenty-page affidavit, which is a real page turner. Who would have thought a woman could get so pissed off by garda harassment and surveillance and . . ."

"And get to the point."

"The point is that this divorce process is well under way and you will lose, there is no surer thing. The next thing you'll get in the post is a hearing date before a judge. That will be the beginning of the end for you."

"I still don't see the point. And I'm losing patience. One more minute and I'm out of here."

"I'm saying that there is a time factor here. Your parole hearing is fixed for eight months' time. You've been a model prisoner, no black marks against your name, but other than that you have nothing to show the parole board. However, if you complete this task I can guarantee it will draw a commendation from some very influential people."

"And you can do that? You can get such a commendation?"

"Yes."

"How?"

"The same way I have you sitting here at three o'clock in the morning."

"There are ways and means?"

"Of course."

"You know a man who knows another man?"

She sighs. "Yes. Mr. Nealon, let's not waste each other's time. We know we can do this dance all night, we both know the steps. I would suggest that you focus on the fact that the completion of this task will enable you to stand in front of the parole board and say, hand on heart, that this is proof of your ongoing rehabilitation, your sincere attempt to purge your guilt. And whether you want to cast all of that as a moving plea or a stirring address is entirely your own choice."

"I will make that speech in any case."

"Yes, but without this task you will stand before the parole board with no leverage whatsoever. Think about it—completing this task and gaining a commendation could gain remission of the last third of your sentence. That might get you out in time to stand up in front of the child custody board and say that you are now an upstanding citizen who has recognized the error of his ways and that you are worthy of an equal share in the care and guardianship of your son." She sits back and gazes at him, then draws the lapels of her jacket around her.

Nealon has seen some things in his time but he has never before experienced such bloodless, equable aggression. Now he sets his whole expression against it, hardening himself. If she notices this, she does not allow it to register in her own face. She nods at him.

"Think about it, Mr. Nealon. With a commendation you could be out of here in two years. That might not be too late to rescue whatever remains of your marriage. Either that or you spend the full remainder of your sentence meeting your son under supervision."

She leans back, her difficult point apparently made. In the lull that follows, Nealon is once more aware of the guard behind him still whistling through his teeth. He is startled to realize that he has been listening to it for quite some time. He cuts off the melody in his head and recalls himself to the issue at hand. His patience is gone and he is washed through with a dangerous surge of anger. The sense of being ambushed and of his own inability to get a decisive grip on the situation now threatens to drive him beyond all caution and careful reasoning. Plus, a sour yeasty rage has bloomed in his belly toward the woman sitting opposite him. He cannot be rid of her soon enough but he knows that they are locked together in this exchange till it concludes. And it will be concluded, whatever that conclusion may be.

When he speaks he finds that without conscious decision he has shifted his defence.

"There is only one flaw in your argument," he declares loudly, "one flaw in all of this. The whole thing is predicated on a false premise: my guilt. You say you read the trial transcript; you must have skipped the page where I pleaded not guilty."

He throws up his hands and declaims in a ringing voice, "I am an innocent man."

"I wouldn't go that far, Mr. Nealon."

"Seven convictions for ID theft—bullshit!"

Her expression does not change but she lowers her voice to a complicit tone. "I agree. Diesel laundering, yes; DVD piracy, yes; cigarettes, yes; but ID theft . . ." she shakes her head. "Mr. Nealon, I have a Rolodex filled with the names of people who can test this game and give me a perfectly good critique—gamers who specialize in all aspects of playability—aesthetics, narrative coherence, historical verity and so on—there is no shortage of such expertise. But none of them will come to the game with your experience, your empathic anger; none of them has your grievance."

Her words are so precisely weighted they threaten to overthrow him completely. He strangles an urge to jab his finger at her but he can do nothing about his voice.

"You know I'm innocent!" he croaks.

The phrase sounds strange in his mouth, more accusatory than he would wish. She concedes nothing in her unblinking gaze.

"You are many things, Mr. Nealon, but innocent is not one of them."

"Fuck that! You know I'm innocent!"

His sudden excitement has him at a loss as to his next move; all he knows is that it demands extreme precision. Sitting back in the chair might lose the moment, something that small. He concentrates on regulating the breath that comes ratcheting up into his throat and he clenches his fists against the urge to reach across the table and grab this woman by the lapels. He sees now that he has misread her from the start: her presence in this cell . . . the task of playing the video game . . . none of this is predicated on his gaming skills, but, incredibly, on his wrongful conviction. His empathic anger . . . his grievance . . . he sees it clearly now and he feels his face broaden out into an expression of disbelief.

"You don't believe it," he says jubilantly, "you don't believe I'm guilty."

The statement hangs untouched in the air between them. Something in the charged excitement of the moment has sharpened Nealon's senses and he registers the smell of expensive skincare products from her. He is surprised—she does not look the type of woman who puts much faith in words like replenish or revitalize. But there it is, there is no mistaking the laminate sheen of her skin. More worrying is the blank expression on her face. Nealon's read on it is that he has not surprised her in any way; she has walked into this cell and seen him react exactly as she has anticipated. No surprises, nothing she couldn't handle. The idea scalds him.

"I'll tell you what I think," he hisses through clenched teeth.

"Yes, tell me what you think." She raises an arch eyebrow.

"I think you are fucking with me," he says softly. "I think you're just dicking me around. You come in here like a dungeon mistress and hand me a list of tasks, asking for all sorts of loyalties in this fucking role-playing fantasy. Well, I don't know who you hang out with but none of this is my idea of fun."

Now she sighs from a deep place within her. "I'm disappointed; I thought we were further along than that, Mr. Nealon."

"This story, this game, it's all bullshit." Nealon swings a wild arm around the room but then instantly looks abashed; the gesture has come off as petulance, not the wrath he'd intended. Neither for one moment does he believe his own accusation, but he does have a confused need to hear her refute it. Something in her denial may reveal what ultimately lies behind all this. Her voice, however, is curdled with sarcasm.

"Yes, Mr. Nealon, I'm fucking with you. This is what my life has come to—driving here in the middle of the night just to sit and fuck with your head. This is my pleasure; this is all I have for doing with my time. And you're right, my boots and whip are just outside the door."

She has given away nothing but when she resumes, her voice is lowered to a savage whisper.

"You can believe what you like, Mr. Nealon. If you want to tell yourself that I am some dried-up bitch, that's fine with me. Or some cunt in a business suit with a castrative glint in her eye— that's fine, too, whatever gets you through this. But remember: you bore me to tears, nothing about you interests me, absolutely nothing. Not the little boy who was brought up in the republican faith on the little Mayo homestead where images of McNeela and Gaughan and Stagg hung beside JFK and Pope Paul VI— nothing about that child interests me. And the same goes for the young man who took a degree in electronic engineering and headed north to do his bit for flag and country—saw a bright future wiring up car bombs and fertilizer bombs; none of that interests me, either. Nor the young man who was hauled into Castlereagh Barracks and was held for forty-eight hours after which he presented at the Royal Hospital with cracked ribs and burst eardrums; he does not interest me. Nor the same man, who shortly after undertook a period of further training in a PLO camp in Libya . . ."

"No!"

"Yes!"

"No, not Libya."

"You're right," she amends, "it wasn't Libya, it was Lebanon, the Bekaa Valley—I thought I'd lost you there for a moment, it must be dull hearing all this, I know I'm fucking bored hearing it myself. But let's keep going, all the things which do not interest me—the same man's return from Lebanon all tooled up with counter-surveillance techniques, just in time for the scaling back of military activities leading into the first ceasefire . . . Then his long period in the wilderness, deployed to south Armagh, to monitor the British army dismantling communication towers. Of course, this may be where the rot set in; this might be where the one true faith got corrupted and you developed a taste for money laundering and commercial diesel. I don't know and I don't care but I imagine if you spend long enough sitting in hail and rain on a ditch with a pair of binoculars, you begin to wonder where your peace dividend is. But I don't care; none of it is of any interest to me. How you lost the faith, what shape or form the dark night of the soul took, the reasons for it and the price you paid for it—none of that interests me, either. Someone looking for a cautionary tale or a parable of the soul's corruption might find use for it. But I'm not that person; I'm not looking for any of that, my needs are a lot simpler. All I know is that this game debuts next month at the Tokyo games convention and the developers want to talk it up in a language beyond the normal vocabulary of these things. That's why I'm here, Mr. Nealon, those are my reasons and nothing more. It's very simple."

She draws a long, tremulous breath; her tour de force appears to have sapped her. Nealon is exhausted, too; hearing his life summarily dismissed like that has stirred up some cloudy sediment in his soul.

"Tell me how it was done?" he asks wearily.

"How what was done?"

Nealon swings a limp arm around the cell. "All this, tell me how I'm serving an eight-year sentence for something I didn't do." He is careful to lower his voice into what he hopes is a conciliatory tone; he spreads his hands in a wide gesture and holds her in an open gaze. "All I know is that I'm at home in my bed when sometime during the night I answer the door to two cops. I'm taken to the station and charged with smuggling and trafficking—DVDs, cigarettes, diesel, the whole lot. It's a clean bust and I figure I'm looking at two to four years. But then everything changes. A detective enters the room and starts questioning me about bank accounts, insurance policies, SSIAs, all these monies routed to an offshore account that has my name and credit history attached. He throws down a list of names and numbers and asks me what I know about them. I tell him I don't know what he's talking about but he has a whole dossier of this stuff with my name all over it. I repeat that I know nothing but he's having none of it. Next thing I'm held on remand and the weeks gradually turn to months— eighteen months, the longest remand prisoner in the history of the state, before I'm eventually brought to trial for seven counts of ID theft for which I draw this eight-year sentence. Now I want you to tell me how that happened."

"What makes you think I know what happened?"

"Because you need my wrongful conviction. I can do without it but your whole reason for coming here is predicated on it. And only that you were certain of it, you wouldn't be here. So you know."

It's very small, the faintest twitch, but he has a definite sense of her stumbling. For the first time he is convinced he has scored a decisive point. Her gaze is crossed with a jittery interference. The feeling intoxicates him, and he decides to go for broke. He waits a moment longer and then rises from the chair.

"Goodnight, it's been nice talking to you."

77

He is two steps from the door when she calls.

"Okay."

"Okay what?"

"I can only guess."

"You'll have to do better than that."

She shakes her head. "Don't overestimate what I know; anything I tell you beyond the basic facts is just reasoned guesswork."

There is a genuine anxiety about her, an obvious fear that she might lose her grip on this entire meeting. For a bewildered moment, Nealon gauges her reaction to be out of all proportion to the risk. But as the moment stretches out, he understands something deeper about her; in spite of what she has said this *is* what her life has come down to, this kind of head fuck. For her, this is its own reward. Nealon sees something conclusive in this woman, something he has never seen before. Everything about her is foreshortened, curtailed; she will perpetuate nothing of herself. It is not something in her accidental nature; it lies deep within her, an essential quality of her being. However present she is in this moment, she is also over and done with, the bitter end, never again . . . She shrugs herself up to her full height and her narrow shoulders open out to disclose a neck with a vivid heat blush near its base, a neck that tapers gently into the hinges of her jaw; all her sleekness toward him now. Nealon reflects that in other circumstances this would be the moment when he would recognize that there is something attractive about her, a glancing promise of erotic violence, something that charges her whole presence. But there will never be any other circumstances, this is all there will ever be between them.

"I need to know; I'm an innocent man."

She guffaws and leans forward on her elbows. "Please, Mr. Nealon, let's quit the bullshit. You are many things but innocent is not one of them. Scapegoat, fall guy, patsy, guinea pig, stooge . . . take your pick, all of these things but none of them innocent."

"What do you mean, stooge, fall guy?"

"Yes, all of those." She draws a long, unsteady breath. "Mr. Nealon, my guess, my belief, is that your conviction was a gesture of good faith on the part of the republican cause. You were offered up and hung out to dry, that's my belief. Before you came to trial it was well known that the Department of Justice needed to frame legislation against the crime of identity theft. At the time, everyone knew it was the coming crime but before they brought you to trial they had no legislation in place with which to fight it. A trial case was needed, a cut and dried case around which they could frame the law. So they went about fabricating it. People were sounded out, meetings took place, anxieties were expressed and hints were dropped. Finally it got to the stage where names were mentioned and it's my guess that it wasn't long before yours was short-listed and you were eventually offered up. And you would have satisfied both sides. Think about it—for all your good work you were only ever a Free State cowboy, you were unspoken for, you were never a made man in the republican family so you never had the kind of immunity which would exempt you from something like this. P. O'Neill didn't lose any sleep about giving you up. And the government was fine with that, also. Your arrest and conviction could be easily sold as long reach and memory. And so you were fitted up. And it was foolproof—the government got the trial and conviction it needed to fine-tune legislation and the Shinners took another step to political legitimacy. Both sides were bound to silence by their involvement."

"There were seven men . . ."

"The seven whose IDs you stole?"

"Yes."

"Seven legends, like Dopey and Sneezy and . . ."

"No!"

"Yes, men in name only."

"Never embodied?"

"Not to my knowledge. Remember their court presence was confined to victim impact statements."

"That was to safeguard their IDs."

"There were no IDs; names, yes but no IDs. I cannot make it any clearer."

It takes Nealon's mind a long moment to close around the distinction.

"A list of names?"

"Yes, just a list, nothing more."

"That's some fix," he breathes.

"It's a piece of work, alright."

"I was convicted of stealing the IDs of seven men who have never existed?"

"That's how I see it."

"I got played."

She cannot hide her disbelief. It takes her about five seconds to lose her hold on a straight face; her features twist down to an expression of savage mirth; she can barely speak for laughing.

"For Christ's sake, Mr. Nealon, didn't you learn anything when you were a foot soldier? Don't tell me you didn't come across this before. Don't tell me you didn't know that in the beginning is the game."

Nealon's shock is so complete he can hardly lift his head to look up; her alarm at losing him completely brings an anxious, conciliatory tone to her voice.

"There's a game out there and the stakes are high. And you never know when you may be asked to step up and play. It could be now, like tonight, or you may go the whole of your life and never be asked or never even know you have played."

Nealon throws up his arms in rage. "Jesus, woman. This is not some grand metaphysical construct—it's a shitty set-up, a betrayal, that's what it boils down to."

"Maybe. But people like you, great transgressors, bring the law into existence."

"Yes and this is the thanks I get."

She shrugs. "People are beholden to you; Nealon versus the state, the case that ring-fenced the sovereignty and integrity of the citizen's identity, people now sleep easier in their beds because of you . . ."

She tires of her sarcasm and sits back in a dismissive slump. "This is all speculation, Mr. Nealon. I'm not saying that this is how it was done, I'm saying that this is one way it might have been done."

"But you're still saying I got played."

"What do you want to hear?"

"The truth."

"Then yes, in the scenario I've outlined, you got played like a penny whistle."

"Just like I'm being played now?"

"No! This is different; now you know the game is afoot, you know the rules and the rewards; how you play is entirely your own decision. But the game is generous; it will accommodate your answer one way or another."

Nealon dearly wants to return to his own cell where he might think over all of this. He is fully aware, however, that any call for a timeout will betray his total confusion. His mind is swamped, adrift in an electric fog. There is also a dryness in his mouth, which is drawing the sap from the rest of his body. He wonders what time it is—dawn is surely breaking beyond the walls of the prison. Just as well the sun is going to come up outside this windowless cell; he has the certain feeling he would ignite in pale flame at the merest touch of sunlight. Olwyn Crayn is sitting in profile, her gaze lost in the depths of the cell wall; when she turns to him, her head comes slowly through a quarter-turn.

"A final thing—you've no idea how complex this game is, Mr. Nealon. This independent studio . . ."

"Studio my arse," Nealon groans, "let's call it what it is, a front, a fucking money-laundering operation, a conduit through which P. O'Neill can reroute funds from any number of scams and present a clean book of accounts at the end of the year; that's what it is!"

"If you say so."

"I do say so!"

She begins again with a show of weary patience. "As I say, you have no idea how complex this game is. Whole departments of philosophy and sociology were placed on retainer as consultants. Cambridge, the LSE, the best brains money can buy. Not to mention all the AI engineers who have worked to perfect a multi-path game that opens out to a series of infinite endings . . ."

Nealon's hand shoots out as if stopping an oncoming vehicle. "Woah, infinite what?"

Olwyn Crayn brightens through her fatigue. "I thought that might grab your attention. Yes, a possibility of infinite endings, each responding and shaped by the character of each game player's mode of playing. This is the Holy Grail of gaming, the first narrative game that is not foreclosed to scripted endings."

Nealon's face clouds in disbelief. She surges on.

"Yes, the first game sensitive to the smallest nuances of each player's moves and open to infinite story paths."

"And this is it?"

"Yes. History can be rewritten here and this is just the beginning, there are plans for other games, other genres: Bloody Friday, the mass escape from the Maze, the Brighton bombing, Hume, Adams . . ."

"The greatest hits?"

"And all the spectaculars."

"And the ten men wasted away in flesh and bone . . ."

"These are the times, Mr. Nealon. There is no principle or sacrifice that cannot be commoditized. All you have to do is map out the co-ordinates of the event and paint it onto a digital chassis. All that remains is to put a price tag on it."

The depth and breadth of Nealon's confusion is now total; he has lost sight completely of what is at stake here and how this meeting ever began. The whole encounter feels like some intricate construct dropped in from a higher, more abstract realm.

"If your story is true, then the people who put me here are the same people I'm going to work for."

"I'm not saying the story is true; it's all speculative, it's full of holes. All I'm saying is that it's one version that accounts for the facts. There may be other versions."

"Suppose we take it as true, why would I help in any way? Why should I help P. O'Neill go legit?"

"That's a stupid question."

"It is?"

"Yes."

"What's stupid about it?"

"I've already given you the answer."

"Give it again, it's way past my bedtime."

"The prize, Mr. Nealon, think of the prize."

Nealon balls his fists on the table and pushes down on them. He does not trust himself any more. The words come through his teeth like ground glass. "You bait me with my son and ask is it worth it!"

"You begged the question, feeling sorry for yourself doesn't work here."

"Is there any version of all this in which I don't get fucked?"

"Maybe, I don't know. As I said, it's all speculation."

"Bullshit!"

"The prize, Mr. Nealon, keep your eye on the prize."

"Fuck you!"

"Goodnight."

"Fuck you!"

With that she rises from her chair and in one continuous movement is gone from the cell. And he is not sure how she's done it but everything remains undisturbed by her going.

Sometime during the last hour or so the guard must have risen from the bunk and left the cell. How could he not have seen him leave, Nealon wonders. But it doesn't surprise him; it's just another detail on the margins of his greater confusion. He leans back and runs his hands through his hair. There is a vicious buzzing in his head, some insect with bladed wings banging around inside his skull. The bottle and stack of cups beside the television catch his eye; he goes over and pours himself a drink of the tepid water. While he's standing, he takes the opportunity to do some stretching exercises. He touches his toes, flexes his arms and rotates his neck. The joints throughout his limbs and back creak with the effort. He sits down and tries to gather his thoughts.

He cannot think but that there is something inevitable here. All of this feels like some fate writ large and undeniable into the very moment and circumstances of his birth. Right now he sees his life as a stumbling ascent through a series of nested, hierarchical games, each with their own traps and hazards, each with their own forfeits, each dangerous to one degree or another. Everything that has led him to this cell now appears as rigid and schematic as a succession of block and lever puzzles, a sequence of pressure locks or hidden keys to be found and turned in the appropriate doors. But vivid as the idea is, Nealon knows that nothing as grandiose as fate or destiny is likely to unfold here tonight. Despite its reach, the immediate scale of all this is intimate, carefully focused. But that does not stop his utter cluelessness bearing down upon him with blunt pressure. Sitting there, he is acutely aware of himself trapped at the vacant core of the prison's cellular bulk, the pale nexus of himself at the heart of its concrete mesh.

He is not as tired as he thought. Something in that woman's going seems to have drawn with it the leaden warmth that so flummoxed him during their stand-off. He has passed beyond fatigue, into that twitchy mode of hyperawareness. There is a rawness also about him, all his senses are alive to the slightest touch; there will be no sleep tonight.

The CD lies on the table. For a long moment he resists touching it; the slightest contact with it might be something from which there is no going back. But Nealon knows that he is playing for time, he knows he is in this to the bitter end. Finally he picks up the disc and places it in the console. He puts on the headset and settles the mic in around his chin as the TV screen comes up with the two-word title, *Homo Ludens*. Drawing a deep breath, he guides the cursor over the title and strikes.

The white screen posts a request to submit a reading for the voice-recognition program. The sample text scrolls up the screen . . . *Recognizing the potential of the current situation and in order to enhance the* . . . He speaks the full ceasefire text through to the end and watches as a field at the bottom of the screen fills up and flashes a line that tells him the voice sample is complete and recognized; evidently the programme is sophisticated enough to extrapolate from these few words. Now the screen lights to a stills montage and immediately any doubts about the game's origins are cleared up. The images morph to life and the whole history of the conflict is collapsed into a two-minute video collage that begins with a clip of the civil rights marches of the late sixties, which fade into running street battles wreathed in tear gas, bodies face down on the city street, the bombed-out buildings and overturned cars, the seething crowds addressed by various demagogues . . . all of this finally giving way to the ranks of black flags and pale crucifixes on walls and gables across a desolate cityscape before the sequence ends on the totemic image of a gaunt Christ figure, wrapped in blankets, behind bars. The whole sequence is underscored by a grating industrial soundtrack, which chimes with the acidic greens and blues that tint the sequence.

After thirty seconds the montage begins to loop through itself once more.

Nealon sits in the gathering stillness, locked in position. A top-down view shows him turned into the television with his legs stretched out in front of him, the wireless control held on his right thigh. He throws his head back and opens his mouth to the heavens—not a howl but a huge yawn, a last surge of fatigue. He pushes himself forward in the chair to rest his elbows on both thighs and to stare at the screen . . . Everything about this scene, the time and place, the lone figure beneath the naked light, the hard geometry of the cell—all these separate elements lend it the most desolate mood of human isolation.

But Nealon's own awareness of himself is on a different scale and in a different register. These are the hours between night and day, that pale interval in which a man's soul might come unmoored. He has a clear sense of this game unfolding all around him, spreading through the dawn outside the prison walls and into the universe beyond. And he sees how every moment of his life is a part of it, every wilful thing he has ever done, every vacant omission, everything he has ever been subject to. And he knows now that no matter what he does, whatever move he makes, he will always be the centre of this game, the soft locus of its infinite attentiveness, the sway of its move and countermove, its eternal sleeplessness. With a sense of the odds stacking against him, he sees how his wife and child are a part of it also, drawn into its spiralling complexity.

And down here, at his level, where player and played are one and the same, he is armed with nothing but his wits; the thought does not reassure him. It is a sudden, intense realization and the force of it makes him acutely sensitive of himself, the gradual morph of his body through each successive moment, the rhythmic rot and renewal of his whole organism right down to the molecular level, the proteins and enzymes of his flesh and bone. An image of himself surging to his feet and bawling out his name and his innocence flits across his vision. But to whom this protest is directed or what he hopes to achieve by it, he cannot say. He draws in his feet and braces them hard on the floor. The moment passes in an electric lurch. He takes the control in both hands. The screen presents two options—*Play* and *Quit*.

Nealon moves the cursor and strikes.

There Are Things We Know

Ever since the death of my father I've slept badly, and my father died twenty years ago . . . that means I've slept badly almost half my life. No matter how deep or peaceful I may be, any untoward sound and I'm bolt upright in a shot, prepared for the worst sort of bad news. So when the knock came to the window that night I was already on the floor and into my jeans with my heart hammering in my chest before the sound had died in my ears. I ran through the hall in my feet and pulled the front door open.

With his shoulder toward me and his face in profile it took me a moment to recognize him. When he turned around and saw my face he took a small step back under the porch light and held up his hands.

"Calm down," he said, "there's no one dead, no one hurt or anything."

It was cousin Davey, a man I hadn't seen in twelve months and yet here he was, on my doorstep at three in the morning telling me everything was okay.

"I thought that was Anthony's room," he added. "I thought that was his room there to the front."

By way of gaining a moment, my heart still hammering in my chest, I put out my hand. He took mine in his and shook it with slow deliberation. However, as genuine and solid as the handshake was, I now felt inexplicably angry. "Davey," I blurted hoarsely, "what's up?"

Davey opened his mouth to speak and seemed to lose the run of himself for a few moments. He uttered a couple of garbled sentences about someone in the car out on the road and then something about someone's *gasúr* . . . and then suddenly he stopped, in a fluster of confusion that was clear now, even to himself. Starting again with a resolute air he began. "Mark, I won't mince words, I'm looking for drink: beer, a bottle of wine, anything." And with that he took another step back under the light.

This was the second week of December, less than fourteen days before Christmas and I knew there was drink in the house. I knew that not two feet away from me in the hall cupboard there were four bottles of wine; I knew also that in the kitchen to my back there was an unopened bottle of Powers. Nevertheless, I shook my head.

"Davey, there isn't a drop here. You know herself, she doesn't like having it in the house."

"Wine, beer, anything," he persisted.

I shook my head, desperately wishing him gone and ashamed of my pathetic lies. "Davey, I'm telling you there isn't a drop in the house, no bottles or cans, nothing."

And there we stood, the two of us locked into this moment of knowing lies and embarrassment. Finally Davey nodded his head and raised his hand. "Sound, Mark, that's fair enough, I'll let you back to bed." He turned and moved off over the gravel and I was relieved to close the door and put out the light.

"Who the hell was that?"

Anthony, my youngest brother, stood in socks and T-shirt at the end of the hall, his face swollen with sleep.

"Cousin Davey."

"Cousin Davey at this hour, what did he want?"

"What do you think he wants? What does he always want at this hour of the night?"

Anthony sighed, I didn't have to spell it out for him. "Was he loaded?"

"Of course he was loaded."

Anthony looked sorrowful and ran his hand through his hair. "He's back on it again, the poor bastard. No one gets this as bad as Davey does; he'll go through the village now tonight looking for drink. I'll bet he'll go over and knock up the uncle."

I remembered the fragile grace with which Davey had moved away from the door, how he had seen through my lies and yet squared with me. I went into my bedroom.

"Don't forget you're giving me a lift into town tomorrow," Anthony called.

"Why am I giving you a lift into town tomorrow?"

"The results of that test, they should be back."

"What's wrong with your own car?"

"I'm leaving her in for the NCT, I told you all this."

"Shite," I breathed, "Okay, give me a shout after nine."

"Make it ten, I have to drive it to the garage at nine. I'll call you when I get back."

"Fine, whatever, Jesus . . ."

I switched off the light and lay on the bed with my hands clasped to my chest, my heart still pounding away like a bastard.

I turned forty over a month ago and that makes me seven years younger than my father was when he died suddenly of a heart attack. For some years now I've been meaning to have a full physical check-up as soon as I struck the big four-oh. I've always had some notion that this marker signalled the end of my youth and now that I was entering the foothills of middle age I needed this check-up to see how I was holding up. And any idea that I might postpone it for a while was done for by a series of heart attacks that had ripped through the family this last year. First up was my uncle, a strong, fit man in his mid-fifties who drove a truck for a builder's yard, a man who never abused himself and whose only vices were a fondness once in a while for twelve-year-old Jameson and a fry. Pushing a lawnmower brought it on. One moment the sun is shining, his family is reared and he's looking forward to spending a week with the grandkids; the next he's under the knife having a stent fitted and his whole life is turned upside down. Two months later his brother in America is walking up the hill to his holiday home in the Catskills when that unmistakeable, clamping pain hits him in the chest.

Quadruple bypass: a dead man walking was how the surgeon described him. That was late autumn but the year had not finished with us. On the phone to her son, an aunt on the same side of the family stops in mid-conversation. Her son on the other end, baffled at the sudden silence, goes, *Mom, what's up, did you have a stroke or something?* And she had, right there holding the phone, just like that. *I knew what I wanted to say,* she would recount later, *but I just couldn't say it. Something was wrong . . .* That stroke required surgery, a procedure that was complicated further when she had a heart attack under the knife. So phone calls were made, a family conference through the wires, and all the menfolk and women got appointments for check-ups. I'd postponed mine for a few weeks. A chest infection had risen into my throat and sent me to a doctor for the first time in years; the antibiotics brought on a dose of diarrhoea, which seriously weakened me, so I had put off the appointment until I got back to something near my normal strength. But today I was in town with Anthony to get the results of his blood test. I saw him now, coming along the street toward the car, a crooked smile on his face. He sat into the passenger side, looked across at me, but said nothing.

"Well," I said, "how long do you have left?"

Quick as a flash, without dropping a beat, he shoots back, "Every day's a bonus from now on." He pulled out a white package. "I'm going to be on these for the rest of my life, my cholesterol is through the roof. So a complete change of diet and I have to be back here in three months."

Anthony was three years old when our father died. To this day I can see him sitting up in bed in his pyjamas, his little face swollen with mumps and him listening to me telling him some bullshit story of how dad was needed in heaven and how he would not be seeing him any more. And if ever I've had to summon up an image of incomprehension, I just think of that swollen, flushed face with those huge eyes staring off into the distance. At twenty years of age that bullshit story was all I could do for him; I had neither the wit nor the wisdom to do any better. But sitting there on the side of the bed, feeding him ice cream to bring down his temperature, I knew well that whatever fathering he was going to get in this life would fall to me. Now, with him sitting there beside me and waving that jar of pills, I didn't care to think what sort of a job I'd done of it.

I was suddenly angry at him.

Over the years Anthony had put on a bit of weight, filled out quickly after his tonsils were taken out at the age of seventeen. He was the heaviest in the family and I worried about him. But this summer I learned there was nothing soft about him. In early June we had cut down a stand of blackthorn that had grown up around the house. It was the first time in years we had worked together like that; five hard days with bush-saws and chainsaws in the hottest spell of the year till at the end of the week we had a big pile of logs stacked at the gable of the shed and a view from the kitchen window that opened out over the hills. And I could hardly keep up with him. In the sweltering heat he had moved easily, wielding the chainsaw lightly in those tight, narrow spaces I could neither reach nor stand in. I saw a toughness in him that I would never have guessed at and I was ashamed of myself for having doubted him. Now, near the middle of December, I saw that week as the happiest spell of the entire year. But right now, with him sitting beside me in the car, I bit my tongue and stayed quiet. He was my youngest brother and worrying me was part of his job. I wasn't going to start on at him because I knew how it would end if I did. I'd lose the head, start effing and blinding, and he'd close up and blank me, stare straight ahead in that stubborn way of his, letting it all wash off him. Someone else would have to talk to him, someone else. So I said nothing, I just started up the car without a word and pulled out into the street.

He kept up the gallows humour that evening—it was just the thing to get a rise out of the mother. He was in the kitchen with one foot up on the chair, lacing his boots before going to work; she was standing over him, drying her hands on a dishcloth, telling him something she needed done for the Christmas.

"You're not listening," she said.

"I'm listening," he replied, without straightening up. "You want the decorations up in the hall and you need a new set of lights for the tree." He stood up and looked at her. "But sure what business would I have putting up Christmas decorations; I'll hardly be around to see ..."

"Anthony!"

"...I'd be better off buying a new suit in case anything happens. I wouldn't want people seeing me lying there ..."

"Stop it!" She swiped him with the dishcloth, and moved to the sink. Anthony pulled his jacket off the back of the chair and turned to me.

"You coming down for one later?"

"Yes," I said, I would be down later; I could do with a pint.

Coming in out of the night air, the warmth of the pub wrapped itself around me. I unzipped the jacket and made for a stool at the centre of the bar. It being mid-December the place was dead, only two other men sitting at opposite ends of the U-shaped bar. I recognized both of them and called their names: Jimmy Lally and Liam Cosgrave. Anthony shoved a pint across the counter to me. On the telly overhead, Sky News was keeping us abreast of the search for Osama. The Yanks were still bombing the caves around Tora Bora, but months on from the start of the invasion there was no sign of the bearded one. The segment ended and the news bulletin cut to the weather.

Anthony spoke in the breathy rasp of an old man. "Set me down there with my dog and my stick, I'd soon find him." He resumed his own voice. "Austie Mangan was in last night looking at that, that's what he had to say, *Set me down there with my dog and my stick ...*"

"He could hardly do any worse," Liam piped from the far end, "and at a fraction of the price."

"The CIA will send for him one of these days, so," Jimmy added from the other end. "Man and dog into the helicopter and off." Jimmy pushed his glass toward Anthony.

"Fudge," Anthony said, laughing over at Liam.

"What?" I'd missed something.

"Fudge," Anthony repeated, "that's the name of Austie's dog, the only one in the house talking to him, he reckons."

"Fudge and Austie in Afghanistan, we could watch them on Sky."

Anthony's been a barman for ten years, ever since his late teens. And he's a good one, and that's something I'm proud of. He has this way with him, knows straight off the customer who wants to talk and knows also the man who has things on his mind and wants to have his pint in peace. He can name everyone in this parish but he's not shy of throwing a few fucks into someone if they're acting up. I've been in enough pubs to know a good barman from the other sort, and while I've seen a few who are as good, I've seen none better.

"You had a visitor last night, Mark," Liam called.

Anthony looked at me. "I was telling the lads about Davey."

"I did, Liam, not the sort I would have wished for."

"You didn't expect that when you opened the door, that apparition."

"No, not that."

I'm ten years older than Liam, went to school with his brother, but sixty fags a day and God knows what amount of drink have driven him into bloated middle age twenty years before his time. Now he held a fag in one hand and clasped his other around his glass. His tone was knowing.

"That's what happens when you start drinking like that in fits and starts—you're out of practice, not thinking. Davey wouldn't have fallen for that a few years ago when he was on it proper; he'd have had a few cans or a bottle stashed away for himself." Liam shook his head ruefully. "You're on it all day and then it's one o'clock in the morning and every place closed—then you're fucked. I know it well, been there many's a time." He shook his head sorrowfully and stubbed out his cigarette.

Liam *would* know these things; he's done more than his share of it. I sat here one night and listened to him tell a story of how he'd been on the beer all day and had decided to go home for a kip in the evening before coming back for the night shift. But when he got home he found the house locked and remembered that the wife and kids had gone to her parents' place for the day. With no key on him he took a walk around the house and found the small window over the bathroom open. Only that he had drink taken he wouldn't have chanced it; he threw the jacket in and followed after it. Shoulders and hips went through easy enough but when he was lowering himself head down between the bath and the toilet, the window shut like a mantrap on his ankle. Three hours he hung there, upside down in the bathroom. By the time the wife came back his head had nearly exploded and the rest of him was blue with the cold. He took an awful dose of the flu and spent a full week in bed with it.

He told that story where he is sitting now and when he'd finished he took a fit of coughing that would have killed a lesser man. He tilted his chin and hauled up a ratcheting series of coughs from the bottom of his lungs, which was painful to hear, his head lowering all the time and his hand locked around the pint on the counter. Worst of all were those long, agonized moments when, caught between coughs, he struggled for air, his tongue rolled outside his lips, going puce in the face, desperately trying to suck air down into his tattered lungs. "Give that man a plunger," someone called. And when he eventually stopped and pulled a hankie out to wipe his eyes, he said that he'd never got over that flu, never shook it; and I would have said there wasn't a man along the counter listening to him who didn't think that flu was the least of his worries.

Liam and Anthony's attention is taken by an ad on the

television. It's one in a new campaign series cautioning the perils of drink-driving. Running in alternate sequences, it shows a little kid playing football in his neat suburban garden, kicking a ball into a goalmouth manned by an oversized teddy; then it cuts to a young man who's scoring a proper goal in some local football match and celebrating afterward, having a few pints with the lads. On his way home he's in flying form, singing along to Fleetwood Mac on the car radio, tapping out the beat on the steering wheel, his mind obviously not on the road.

Of course the inevitable happens: the car hits the kerb, veers out of control and bursts through a flimsy timber fence; between crushed flowers and tumbling cars and screaming kids the child footballer lies dead on the lawn: the child's father rushes out, picks up the prone body and sinks to his knees, crying out to the heavens. The ad ends with a white text on a black screen: "Could you live with the shame?" I haven't seen it before and it's undeniably good. The lingering mood is sombre, admonitory, and it carries real weight in the quietness of the bar. Liam, however, is having none of it. He gestures at the screen.

"That wouldn't have happened if your man had a right wall there. A timber fence is no good. Blocks on their flat, that's what he should have had there."

Laughter comes choking up into my throat and I leave down my pint. Inside the bar Anthony has his head lowered over the tap, his shoulders rocking with mirth. Liam pushes his glass toward the centre of the bar, the devil's grin on his face.

"Put a last one in that, A; we'll fuck off home to our beds, then."

Anthony locked the door, pulled down the blinds and I helped him stack the chairs on the tables. Now that the place was cleared, we were going to have a last pint together.

"It was very quiet tonight."

He reached for a glass. "It'll be like that for another week. Besides, cops were pulling at the bridge last night and on the Westport road two nights ago. People are afraid to come out, even if it's only for a few pints."

"It's not worth chancing it."

"No, it's not. And this place is a soft touch, the cops rack up the numbers of arrests and don't give a shit. Half the charges are thrown out in court, then, for one reason or another. It's a pure farce." He placed two pints in front of me and ducked out under the counter. "Jimmy Whelan was the best I ever saw. Jimmy would come in here and have the craic and drink ten, twelve pints and walk out as sober as he came in, no piss or nothing." He pointed to a table in the middle of the floor. "The cops came in one night and told anyone with cars to put their keys on the table there. Jimmy finished up his pint and pushed past them to the door. *If you think I'm walking out that bollocks of a road at this hour . . .* They let him go as well and of all the men coming and going that road he was never caught."

"He went fast in the end, though, the same Jimmy."

"He did, he got a heart attack in the house, the brother found him the following day."

We've done this before, had these pints after closing time and I enjoy them like no other. Here in the quiet warmth, with the lights dimmed, there is a type of contentment you can't get anywhere else. Man to man, putting the world to rights, getting on that blissful buzz when the world and everything in it becomes coherent—there's nothing like it. In this mood and these hours nothing is impossible.

A couple of years back, before he took to sea in a trawler and worked on construction, Anthony ran his own pub just up the street. Within a year, he turned an old man's pub into the kind of place where young surfer dudes stood shoulder to shoulder with old sheep farmers in the middle of a concrete floor. He met his figures plus fifteen percent and gained listings in two tourist guides as one of the best licensed premises in Ireland. And late at night, after he'd cleared the place and swept the floor, we'd do exactly as we're doing now; sit alone in the dim light, talking football and movies and books, listening to music. Hank and John Denver were the big favourites at that hour of the night: *Some days are diamonds . . .*

> *Some days are diamonds*
> *Some days are stones*
> *Some days the hard times*
> *Won't leave me alone.*

We'd play that song over and over, singing along to the chorus, giving it loads, and I remember those nights lit with such unlikely well-being that it would have been almost foolish to acknowledge it.

"So the pig is barred," he says suddenly, "I can't go the pig."

"What?"

"The diet, the doctor says I need to have a whole change of diet. Anything to do with the pig is out. So it's rabbit food from now on."

"That'll be tough. Did he say anything about getting up off your hole and doing some exercise?"

"I've sorted that out. Liam was telling me before you came in that he's starting groundwork on those houses across from us in the New Year. He asked me would I be interested. I said sound, there's four months' work in it, just hop across the fields to it in the morning. It beats driving in and out to Galway for the same thing."

"Is he any good at that sort of thing, is he tidy?"

"He's tidy and he's tasty," Anthony said, "you mightn't think to look at him but he leaves neat work behind him. Kerbing, manholes, paving, he does all that groundwork and as long as it doesn't rise above the window sill he's fine—same as myself, though, he has no head for heights."

I know that sometime in the past Anthony has taken a fall off a roof. He never told me but I learned it from one of the lads. From what I know, he was fixing lead flashing around the base of a chimney when he lost his footing; he tipped back off the apex of the gable into the blue air and landed, by the grace of God, flat on his back in a pile of sand. The thought of it makes me weak and although I've never asked him about it, I do know that it put an end to him doing any work on roofs or scaffolding or anything that rose above his own head. Soon after that fall he took to the bay in a 25-foot trawler.

"And he has a great head as well, he can size up a job in an instant," he continued solemnly. "When we had that job in Barna we had six houses on one side of a cul-de-sac, the other six were given over to some crowd from Connemara. One day during lunch break Liam goes over to see how the other lads are getting on. He's gone about twenty minutes and when he comes back to the hut he's bursting his arse laughing. *We'll have a few more weeks here yet*, he says—*when the engineer comes tomorrow he'll pull up every bit of work they've done.* And that's exactly what happened. The engineer came the next day, took one look at their work and ran the lot of them: steps where there shouldn't be steps, manholes where there should be water-traps, inclines running the wrong way, the whole thing upside down and back to front . . . one glance and Liam saw it all—we had another two months' work there. That same evening he was pushing a barrow with a few paving slabs in it. One of the lads up on the scaffold calls down to him, says, *Come on to fuck, Liam, put a few more slabs in that barrow.* Quick as lightning Liam shoots back, *My ears are on the side of my head boy, not on top of it . . .* That quietened the buck . . . Wasn't that a good one? *My ears are on the side of my head . . .*"

Anthony doesn't know it but this is something he takes from dad—an ear for the keen phrase, the mimicry, the joyous telling of these tales. In no other way does he so completely resemble him. None of the rest of us—my other brother or sister—has his gift for it. He comes home at night and I say to him, *Any craic?* That's enough to start him off. Young and all as he is, he must have a thousand stories already.

Now he throws back the last of his pint and gathers up the glasses. "Will we have a short before we go or will we leave it at that?"

I take up my jacket. "Let's leave it at that. I'm driving back in the morning."

"Sound."

We walk down the empty street together, out over the bridge and through the crossroads. The house is three minutes up the road and when we get around the back we stand for a while, pissing off the walk into the grass. A small moon hangs over the village and we can see across the dark hills as far as the Reek on one side, Mweelrea on the other. Rain begins to fall, one of those light mists that drifts by in the moonlight. Anthony is zipping himself up and chuckling away.

"Jimmy told a good one this evening before you came in: how he lost a field of silage earlier this summer. How did you manage that, I asked. Jimmy grinned and said, *I left it to God and God left it to me and between the two of us we lost it, that's how.*

We laugh and stand there a moment and, with nothing more to be said, we open the back door and turn into the house.

• • •

So we've made it to Christmas and we're walking the beach beyond the town. This is our new health regimen: exercise and diet. Santa's brought me a new pair of boots and they're stiff on my feet so I'm breaking them in over even ground. It's a beautiful day, one of those clear sharp days that thrills you deep in the bone, makes you feel properly alive. Our goal is half a mile distant, a small stream running to the sea, marked out by a large rock; overhead a watery sun is doing its best.

"Look who's coming," Anthony says.

There's a lot of people on the beach: kids playing football; couples; dogs. Up ahead a young fella is leaning back, taking the strain from a huge kite high above. It looks like nice work—even at this distance I can feel the draw in his arms, the pull in the small of his back.

"Uncle T, out walking as well."

I see him now, coming toward us with his hands thrust into the pockets of his jacket. Another moment and he spots us.

"It's no use standing up, lads," he calls cheerily, "you have to keep walking, you won't do it standing up."

We shake hands and wish him happy Christmas and he's in flying form. His family is down for the holiday, his two girls with husbands and kids and his only son back from Jersey. We talk and make plans to meet up later that night for a drink. After a few moments we move off in opposite directions.

"What the hell's a stent, anyway?" I ask, "do you know what it is?"

Anthony nods. "Yes, he showed me a leaflet in the house. You wouldn't believe it; it's like shuttering in your arteries, keeping it open."

"That'll put an end to John Jameson."

Anthony looks at me like I've said something stupid. "He

doesn't care, he told me himself. He said life is too sweet, his family is reared, there's just himself and herself; it's not too much now to look after his health. He's talking of getting a taxi licence."

"He can't drive a truck but he can drive a taxi, how does that work out?"

"Fucked if I know, some sort of insurance thing, I think."

We turn at the rock and put the low sun behind us. Now we're going in the right direction. The summer before he died, myself and my father were on this same beach together. It was a Sunday—it had to be or we wouldn't have been here. I was after coming out of the water, drying in the sun, and we were talking about something or other when, out of the blue, he challenges me to a sprint.

"Come on," he says, "as far as the rock," his face keen with the sudden idea of it.

My heart sank. I was nineteen that summer and fitter than I'd ever been. I was playing senior football with the parish team and I'd had county trials earlier that year. He was forty-six and I didn't want this challenge but what could I do? He took off his shoes and socks and rucked up the ends of his trousers and we stood side by side. He leaned forward then and called it: Ready, Steady, Go! He had eaten up two whole strides before I'd put a foot forward, running with a rigid, upright stride that carried him lightly over the sand, his elbows pumping, his shirt swelled out across his back. I surged off and drew beside him at the halfway mark, all my reluctance swept aside by the savage competitiveness that was my way in these things. I pulled ahead of him, one stride, and said now I'll burn him off, fuck it. But that one stride was all I managed, not another inch, no matter how hard I pumped or how deep down I reached—not another inch. We drew up at the stream and he was breathless and laughing his head off, his face broad with glee. I couldn't understand it at first but after a moment I thought I knew: he was glad, glad for both of us, glad I'd won and glad that he'd made more than a fight of it. I tried not to sound surprised.

"I never knew you were that fast."

He continued laughing and turned toward the sea, hauling in deep breaths. "Not running," he said, "handball was my game, doubles; myself and Peter Burns, we were never beaten."

Six months later he would die in his bed, home after a few pints in the same pub Anthony would manage fifteen years later. He went to bed with the paper and sometime in the middle of that night our bedroom door burst open and our mother came through shouting, *Get up, get up lads, there's something wrong with Daddy!* I charged through the hall after my brother, into their bedroom, and saw him lying on his back, his face blue and him gasping for air. I turned back out of the room, pulled on my boots and jacket in the kitchen and set out into the pissing night to run the quarter of a mile into the town to get the doctor. When I got back he was dead.

I haven't told Anthony any of this and I'm not going to tell him today. Someday yes, but not today. This is Christmas and today is about walking, keeping these dodgy hearts of ours ticking over; stories like that can hold for another time, for some night after hours when they're really needed. Anthony's mobile goes off in his pocket and he pulls it out and holds it to his ear.

"Sound," he says, "about fifteen minutes." He turns to me. "Let's speed it up, the dinner's on the table."

We pick up the pace for the final stretch, lengthening our stride and feeling the cold, sharp air reach down into the bottom of our lungs.

These Two Men

They came today, knocked on my door around mid-morning, and when I opened it they told me without any preamble that I was dead.

There they stood in the hallway, their bland interchangeable faces glowing in the half-light, these two men, these bearers of the worst possible news. And as I stood there I realized there was no doubting them; they already had a rooted, immovable presence and their open-shouldered stance blocked off the entire corridor. And yet I had no fear. On the contrary I found myself swept up in a sudden lightness of spirit that coursed through me, a blithe expansiveness of mood that had me inviting them into my flat. I stood back and motioned toward the sofa under the window where I might get a better look at my two visitors, these two sudden men.

They came as a pair—this much was immediately evident.

Both wore suits and were clean-shaven and I guessed there was about ten years between them; the older one, the heavier one who had given me the bad news in the hall, I judged to be around my own age; his partner, I put in his late twenties. Both appeared to have mastered the paradox of establishing a solid, physical presence while at the same time effacing any specific detail in which this presence might be grounded. *They were clean-shaven, they wore suits*—that was as much as I would ever be able to say about them. And yet there was something of the comic double act, also, a complementary ease in the way they sat there, which convinced me I was about to witness one of those deft, professional routines that was no doubt worn smooth and seamless by much time and practice. And as I stood there gazing at them, I reflected that this was something new; I had not lived the sort of life that drew men in suits toward me; uniforms yes, suits no.

"So," I said airily, "in what way am I dead? Spiritually perhaps, possibly metaphorically: What way exactly?" I was in unexpectedly good form.

All promise of light comedy evaporated completely in the toneless delivery of the older man. He leaned forward with his elbows on his knees and his voice came across like dry sand running in a pipe. "It would be a mistake to understand yourself dead in any partial, metaphorical or analogical sense," he began. "There is only one way in which someone is dead and that is literally, totally and absolutely. Such is the case with you at this very moment. And, I would advise, the sooner you dismiss all evidence which says otherwise, the sooner we will all be able to move on." He sat back and placed both his hands on his knees.

By rights a fit of laughter should have taken hold of me then. The ludicrousness of what he had just said was verified in every atom of my being; in fact my whole circumstance at that particular moment could hardly have served a more vivid testimony to my life and its ongoing continuance. For starters there was this pain in my lower back, which throbbed warmly after I had slept awkwardly on it; the apple I had eaten for breakfast had lodged a nagging piece of itself between my teeth and would not come loose; not ten minutes ago I had hung up the phone on my girlfriend and earlier still, I remembered, I had made plans to meet a friend for a drink that night; my leg . . . I caught myself on abruptly. That I had been pushed so easily into this survey of myself and my circumstances says something of my visitors' confidence in themselves and my own aptness for confusion. I actually found myself stammering and asking for some further evidence to support their outlandish claim.

The older of the two went to the table and spread across it a series of pale documents; he did this with such economy of move-ment that it flummoxed totally whatever understanding I might have had of them. To my bewildered gaze there appeared to be a series of spiralling figures and indices, endless columns of data and other graduated observations, all waxing and waning and spiralling across six or seven sheets of ruled paper . . . Somewhere amid these convulsive figures I thought I glimpsed something of a life's ineffable fleetness but I could not be sure of this. Before I had grasped the idea clearly, I was distracted by the younger man who, till now, had busied himself looking out the window. Now he turned to me with a wan smile.

"It could be worse," he said evenly, "it could be a lot worse."

He gazed round at the flat, appearing to turn a full three-sixty without moving his feet and as he did so I had an unnerving sense of displacement; it was as if I was seeing not just the room with his eyes, but also the life it inscribed. I found myself acutely ashamed of the worn furniture and general shabbiness of the whole place. There did not appear to me a surface or appliance that was not stained or grimy in one way or another. Indeed, it appeared to me as if the entire flat was held together by stains and scuffmarks. Everything looked unspeakably dreary in the grey morning light and I had no doubt but that it smelled, also. What sort of a life was responsible for that kind of shabbiness, what sort of life passed through these rooms and left behind such filth? I realized that the question was not properly my own or wholly rhetorical but that it belonged to the younger man at the window. It was as if I was hearing his voice inside my head; his dull reproving tone. "Look at yourself," he was saying, "pushing forty and nothing to show for it. No wife or child, nothing completed or finished; one project after another aborted or abandoned in one fashion or other; nothing but false starts, revisions and amendments. Furthermore, there is neither family nor loved ones to grieve for you." He spread his hands wide in a gesture of finality. "You've had your chance and you've wasted it and when all is said and done you will be no great loss, least of all to yourself."

Being spoken to like this in your own kitchen should rouse an ordinary man to a fit of righteousness. But it seemed that their power over me was so absolute I was completely incapable of any proper response to his charge. And so smooth was their dismantling of my psyche that I began to suspect there was something uncanny about them both. Now, what had appeared at first to be a deft routine with all the sheen and polish of professional repetition, might in reality be the seamless, unhesitant unity of a single being. The sinuous ease with which they picked up each other's thoughts and this tendency of one to absent himself in the background while the other spoke had me wondering if, in fact, these two men were not conjoined in some mysterious way beyond ordinary comprehension.

After dwelling uneasily on this for what must have been

several moments, I was brought back to the situation in hand by the giddy realization that, incredibly, I was being offered a job of some sort—or, more accurately, I was being recruited to some sort of organization. The older of the two was now addressing me and had begun wooing me with a distinctly backhanded compliment. The thrust of it was that while he recognized I had proved to be an indifferent *living* man, he had no doubt, and indeed some confidence, that I would prove to be *a very good dead man*, whatever that might be. Indeed, he went so far as to say that, contrary to all appearances, my life had not been a complete waste of time and that, in more than one instance, it had served evidence that hinted strongly that I might be the very man they were looking for.

What evidence, I wanted to know.

"Your politics, for instance," the younger one said.

I guffawed and shook my head happily, glad to have any small advantage over them—nothing was too trivial at this stage.

"I have no politics," I declaimed stoutly. "I have never voted nor do I have any party affiliations."

"We know that," the younger one said, "but you have taken up several reasoned positions. Your attitude to Cuba and North Korea, your implacable opposition to totalitarianisms, left or right . . ."

I guffawed once more, now gathering in confidence. "And I get a prize for that? Since when did drink-talk become a 'position' or indeed 'implacable opposition,' for that matter?"

"It all becomes part of the wider configuration. There was also your support for the second invasion of Iraq; your heroic vigil in front of Sky News was noted. And there was that incident at the funeral of your friend's father. Your defence of coalition forces was noted and appreciated."

"What defence?"

"You had a series of bitter exchanges with a young German woman. Several people commented on it—it soured the atmosphere of the gathering; eventually, a friend of the deceased had to separate the two of you."

I remembered the funeral vividly. It had happened over six months ago, the father of a friend dying after a long illness. I had taken the early train and arrived at the funeral service flustered and regretting the Death's Head T-shirt I had pulled on so hurriedly that morning. And later that evening, sure enough, I seemed to have some dim recollection of a heated argument with someone whose constant refrain of "People like you make me laugh" had made me especially angry. I remembered it being late at night and that I had stood with my back braced against the bar for fear I might fall over while the thread of what passed for my argument unravelled hopelessly . . . But, of course, it may have been somewhere else, some other gathering entirely.

"Furthermore," the young man was saying, "while keeping a close eye on their development you have prudently withheld judgment on recent events in Venezuela. This caution is to your credit."

Till now the naked, irrefutable fact of their presence in my flat had blinded me to the obvious question of who these men were and who had sent them. Now it seemed certain to me that they had come from the New World and were probably two field agents from one of those security agencies that had performed so abysmally in recent years. They looked like security agents and they behaved as I imagined security agents should behave. And yet it seemed incredible to me that there were men in that distant jurisdiction, important men working in remote areas of government who had evidently taken an interest in me and my life and had despatched these two to sound me out. It seemed not only incredible but also hopelessly trivial, evidence that someone somewhere had been sidetracked. Nevertheless, there were those

suits and those haircuts and those mechanically arch enuncia-
tions ... I made an effort to concentrate harder.

"There are certain things we don't know," the older man admit-
ted, "certain limits to our knowledge."

"Yes."

"Gaps," the younger man clarified.

"Gaps?"

"Yes."

"We want to commission a report," the older one elaborated.
"There are clear gaps in our knowledge of certain things and as
such they present a very real security risk. The man who would fill
these gaps with accurate accounts and reasonable guesstimates
would have the entire world beholden to him."

"What sort of report?"

"A reconnaissance report. You would be fully briefed and
equipped and pointed at the target; certain back channels would
then be open to you. Our specific interest is in scale drawings,
schematics, architects' blueprints if at all possible. You would be
asked to make note of the outlying topography and whatever
early-warning systems are in place. Certain evaluations would
also be helpful—estimates of manpower, ordnance and readiness
for conflict ..." He continued on in this vein for some time and
as he did so an overwhelming sense of fatigue took hold of me,
a dry falling sensation as if some ashen sediment were settling
down through my limbs and torso.

Had he not eventually mentioned something about being
put on a generous retainer he would have lost my attention
completely. Now he assured me he had access to limitless funds
but stressed that it was in everyone's interest that my presence be
buried in the deep end of some discretionary budget—that way I
would be shielded from all oversight and accountability. Furthermore, everything about me would be deniable, all my actions

and whereabouts, my very existence. In the unlikely event of my capture they would deny all knowledge of me and I would leave no trace whatsoever. Looking at them, I did not doubt from their blank faces that these men could arrange all this.

"It sounds dangerous."

"You can take our word that for someone like you it presents no danger at all."

Why I should take their word or anything else they had to offer was something I never thought to question.

"This target, what sort of a thing is it? Is it a place or a thing?"

"It is both a place and a thing."

"It's a compound or an installation of some sort?"

They shook their heads in unison and said that they could not be more specific at this time; all information from here on would be available on a need-to-know basis. I understood. They were right. I did not need to know: certainly not right now, and maybe not ever.

Now that I had so much to think about, I was keen they should leave and, as if sensing my patience was at an end, they began gathering up their papers; the older of the two handed me a card on which there was a telephone number. The atmosphere in the room now was perfectly amiable, as if some difficult piece of business had been settled to the benefit of everyone.

As they made ready to go, there ensued what may have been the oddest moments of the entire episode. In this relaxed mood, we found ourselves engaged in pleasant banter, which skipped through several topics—the weather, recent political events and last of all, and by way of winding things up, the football championship. All three of us were agreed that, so early in the year, it was difficult to call the championship—as things stood there were at least six teams in with a chance. I advanced a case for my own county and was listened to attentively—we had done well in the league and some promising newcomers had strengthened what was already a gifted panel; all in all I was hopeful and I thought my voice and argument sounded authoritative in the room.

My speech, however, had a curious effect on the younger man; in one moment he seemed to lapse from himself completely into a twitchy and fretful version of the smooth professional who had till now so easily commanded his role and space in the room. Bracing both hands on the back of the chair, he lowered his eyes and shook his head dubiously. While he conceded we had motored along well enough in the league—that was his phrase, *motored along*—and we were definitely as strong as any through the middle of the field, he doubted our ability to move up into a championship gear; he couldn't see it happening. He dwelt critically on the fact that the first instinct of our playmaker was to take a step backward while sizing up the available options, and only then lay on thirty-yard cross-field passes onto the forward's chest. This was well and good, the young man conceded, on heavy winter pitches, but would it translate to the quicker surfaces of summer? He wondered if the ball wouldn't go in too slow to the forward—a better option, he opined avidly, would be to drive the ball quickly into the open space behind the defence so that when the forward ran onto it he would be facing the goal. Furthermore, he did not think converted basketball players made good midfielders—it spoils for the other game, he said. However, he conceded, all things considered it might indeed be our year and if it was, it wouldn't be before time, and there wouldn't be a man or woman in the country who would begrudge us because . . .

He stopped as suddenly as he'd begun and seemed altogether sheepish, as if realizing this speech had been the most embarrassing sort of incontinence. Such was his sudden gloom that I thought he must surely have some investment in his argument above the merely theoretical. I saw that there was a muscular girth to him and that the span of his two hands covered the back of the chair completely; it was easy to imagine him being secure under a high ball and for more than one moment I was lost in speculation that he might be the answer to an ongoing weakness in our right corner . . . The effect of this outburst on his older partner was of a subtler, more drastic sort. Something like a grimace of despair crossed his face, an expression so rapidly erased I could only think that this was not the first time it had happened; evidently, the young man's speech had disclosed something, which, while hardly fatal to their purpose, was definitely not to their credit. Once again the conviction that I beheld a single, unified being came to me, but the possibility of ever seeing one without the other now presented itself in the same degree of improbability as a square circle or a single-sided coin.

Their grace and assurance was completely gone. The young man's speech hung in the room as a gross error. It had opened a mood of embarrassment that turned quickly to something bleaker, less forgivable. If our meeting had drawn us together into some delicate, nuanced complicity, a virtuoso construct in which each had ably played his part, now, because of the young man's outburst, it all lay in ruins. Visibly anguished, the older man made haste to draw his younger colleague through the door; he followed awkwardly behind, knocking his briefcase against the chair and pulling the door too heavily behind him.

Alone in the room, I was surprised by the sour feeling of disappointment that took hold of me. It came as a real shock to realize that in spite of everything I had enjoyed my two visitors, most especially the arcane expertise they had brought with them. There was no denying that their silken performance had spoken to my vanity; whoever had sent them had seen fit to deploy two men who, for so long, had appeared to be at the top of their game. But the young man's callowness had ruined that and this angered me. Moreover, it cast considerable doubt on my belief that they had come all the way from the New World; it seemed unlikely that the young man's acute analysis, his fluent handling of a cultural idiom, had its origins anywhere other than some place close to home. Nevertheless, I felt sorry for him. Outside, out of earshot, I imagined he would be severely rebuked by his older colleague and possibly gain some sort of written reprimand; it seemed likely that whoever these people were they would surely do these things by the book.

When they had left, I sat looking at the card I held in my hand—a plain white thing, which carried nothing save a ten-digit mobile phone number. Would I ever call it? I had no immediate intention of doing so. After a while I went into the kitchen and spent several vexed minutes vainly trying to twist the tap tight enough to make it stop dripping. I crossed back into the sitting room and lay down on the sofa. After what seemed like only a short time I woke up and, after consulting my mobile phone, found I had in fact slept for five hours and that my back had twisted itself into a new and more exquisite variant of the pain I had suffered since getting out of bed.

I thought back over the morning. Of all the stored impressions I had of it, one detail in particular presented itself with vivid insistence—this alleged argument I was supposed to have had with the German woman. Nothing about it seemed improbable—if anything, it seemed all too like me; the drink, the late night, the heated debate, the tendency toward righteous homily—I have a long history of this kind of thing. And yet, for the life of me, I could not put a face to her. Who was she, what exactly had I said to her? I was anxious to get this straightened out because I had some notion that in doing so the wider events of the morning would come into clearer focus.

So I reached for the phone and called this friend of mine. Two, three times I called but his phone kept ringing out; I would have left a message but his voice mail was off. I'd call again later on. I sat for a long time on the sofa listening to the tap dripping in the kitchen and dismally resigned myself to the fact that it would have to stay that way for the time being because, having no tools or washers, there was nothing I could do about it.

And as the minutes passed, I gave myself over completely to a blunt feeling of disgust at having wasted what promised in its first hours to be a perfectly good day.

From the
City of Dolls

If you ever go looking for this pub, here's where to find it. Come off the Charles Bridge into Karlova, pass the torture museum and turn right into Liliova. It's the first of three pubs on this short street, you'll find it behind heavy wooden shutters under a yellow Gambrinus sign. During my stint there as a regular, it played home to a crowd of hard-drinking expats, mainly British IT workers and American real estate sharks who'd been lured to the city on foot of a property boom that was just going into decline when I got there.

One afternoon I gathered up my newspaper to make space at the table for a beautiful woman in her early twenties who had materialized above me. Her height and bone structure were an immediate giveaway. Cheekbones, a former girlfriend had assured me, Slavic women have these great cheekbones. Whatever about cheekbones, six weeks' casual observation in pubs and on the streets had convinced me that, should the need ever arise, the world could draw on this city's standing army of lingerie models and off-duty action-movie heroines. Pulling off her coat, this particular one motioned to my copy of *The Guardian*.

"You are English?"

"No, Irish."

She smiled keenly. "Sorry."

"It's okay, we can start again."

Beneath her coat she wore a scoop-necked T-shirt over a grey skirt and black tights. My gaze snagged at the top of her left breast where there appeared the scaly sheen of what I took to be scar tissue; during the next few minutes I tried not to stare at it. She stirred her coffee, turned toward me and we fell to an easy and relaxed conversation. I told her my reasons for being in the city and she told me about a waitressing job and English lessons across the river in the Berlitz School. Then, without warning, she paused in mid-sentence, dipped her head into both hands and yawned hugely.

"I'm so tired," she said, surfacing abruptly and shaking her head. "I slept badly. The phone ringing all night, my flatmate is having trouble with her boyfriend." She yawned again and then added dozily, "But at least I didn't faint like I used to."

I was flummoxed—phone calls and fainting—I couldn't see the connection. Before I could say anything she went on, speaking now in the distant tones of one who was recalling some absent version of herself with more than a trace of bemusement.

"When I was a child I used to fall down in a faint whenever I got a fright: doorbells or sudden crashes or even someone coming up behind me and tickling me . . . down I'd go. But I wasn't the only one—my mother and older sister did the same thing." She tapped her chest with a narrow index finger. "It's a heart condition, a weakness which causes it to shut down whenever its rate rises suddenly . . . It closes down, shuts off the blood supply to my brain and I would fall to the ground in a faint." She shrugged. "It was just a part of my childhood, something I did, something we all did, as a matter of fact. One day the phone rang in our flat and myself and my sister stood there and saw each other's eyes roll up into our heads before we passed out. My mother, in the next room, came in and pulled the fruit bowl off the kitchen table on her way to the floor. That evening my father came home and found the three women in his life lying in a heap. Two months later he took off to a clerical job in a lignite mine in Slovakia." She screwed her face into a querulous frown, "High maintenance, you use that phrase?"

"Yes, we use that phrase."

"Well that's what we were, three high-maintenance girls."

"Three women," I blurted, "three women falling down in a faint . . ."

"Yes, three women, you can read all about us in medical journals, we're well known in the cardiac community. And my mother is the one with the looks, by the way, my sister and I are only so-so."

I didn't remember arguing the point. By now she'd emptied her cup of coffee so I called her another and a second beer.

"It is allowed," I stumbled, "all that caffeine . . . ?" I motioned vaguely with my hand.

"Yes, it's okay." She touched the scar tissue above her breast. "In the early nineties this new technology was developed and my mother and sister were among the first to be fitted with it. It's an electrical device, it kicks in with two hundred and fifty volts whenever your heart rate falls below a certain threshold."

"Like a jumpstart," I said.

"Yes, like a jumpstart. I was only sixteen at the time and they didn't know whether it would be safe to fit one for me—no one so young had had it done before. But my fainting fits were becoming more frequent and the periods of unconsciousness were getting longer and longer. They were afraid I might fall down one day and not wake up. So, shortly before my seventeenth birthday, I had this thing fitted in my chest."

She reached over and took my hand. Hers was cool and dry, as if it had just been dipped in talc.

"You can feel it here."

She pressed my hand to the top of her left breast, making it yield under the firm pressure. Pressing hard on my index finger, she ran it up and down beneath the seam of her T-shirt. Something wouldn't yield; a narrow rib, thicker than an artery but with a synthetic hardness, ran vertically from beneath her collarbone, then seemed to sink behind the mass of her breast. Feeling that synthetic hardness beneath her warm flesh, my mind was crossed with a crazy and complete thought—this is how you turn into David Cronenberg, I said to myself, my head is going to explode any moment.

"I'm proud of my scar," she said, releasing my hand. "Four or five teenagers have gone on to have this implant. But I was the first."

The warmth of her breast hummed on my fingertips; it took me a moment to gather my thoughts.

"It must affect your life, there must be so many things you cannot do?"

She was now openly enjoying my astonishment; her smile broadened.

"I have this little manual," she said, "all the things I cannot do. Cycling up hills, sprinting, swimming . . . it's a long list but as yet I've never tripped it. My mother has, though. One day we were hurrying to catch the Metro in Malá Strana, walking quickly, not running. I was two paces ahead of her at the top of the stairs when she called out to me. When I turned around, she was sinking to her knees against the wall. Then it kicked in. Have you seen the movie *Blade Runner?*"

"Yes."

"That scene where Harrison Ford . . ."

"Deckard."

"Deckard, yes, that scene where Deckard hunts down the replicant and she lies dying in the rainy street, kicking her life out. That's what it was like for my mother that day, really scary. She was thrown to the ground, kicking, trying to tear open her blouse. I stood over her trying to keep people away from her. You cannot touch her because she is . . ."

For the first time she faltered over a word. After a moment's hopeless groping she gave up and held up her hands beseechingly.

"Live?" I said.

"Yes, live, that's the word, electric. She was very embarrassed but she recovered and that was the main thing." She fell silent for a moment and when she spoke again her voice had a different, giddier timbre to it. "But there is one way of tripping it that I would like to experience . . . if you make love very hard it trips the mechanism and all that electricity . . . the man is supposed to find it very pleasurable." She was looking me straight in the eye now and to my shame I found that I was less a man of the world than I had thought.

"But," she said with a sharp giggle, "my boyfriend tries very hard."

I lowered my head to let a complex wave of embarrassment and disappointment pass through me; when I looked up she was on her feet wrapping her scarf around her. I heard myself offering to pay for her coffee and I heard her thanking me. She wished me luck and, shouldering her bag, she moved off between the tables to the door.

Fifteen minutes later I stepped out into the leaden day, my

head still swimming with what I'd just heard. I walked back through Liliova and turned right under the astronomical clock. Halfway across the old square I pulled up and looked around me, suddenly feeling very foolish . . . Of course! How could I have missed it?—this city of dolls and mechanicals, this city of robots and golems . . . what else would you meet but an electric woman?

As I stood there laughing I became aware of the cold and pulled my coat up around my ears. It was the middle of the afternoon, grey skies snagged in the steeples of the cathedral. The crowds drifted through the square. Three months from now this city would throng with German and Japanese tourists making its narrow streets unpassable; coming here in winter had been one of my better ideas. And turning a full three-sixty, watching all those women move smoothly over the cobbled paving in high heels and short skirts, fading into the grey light, I thought then what I now know—that if I lived to be a thousand I would never visit another city with such a company of tall, beautiful women.

Six weeks later, back home, I stood at the bottom of my garden feeding page by page a sizeable manuscript into a small fire. All curdled inspiration and nonsense, every page of it hopeless whimsy, the work of ten weeks. And as I stood there peeling off the pages and dropping them into the flames, I thought back to that young woman in the pub. And the thing that came back to me clearest of all wasn't what she'd told me or the strangeness of what she'd told me. No, what came back to me clearest of all was the fact that one day in a strange city a beautiful woman stepped in out of the cold, in out of the blue, sat down beside me and told me a story. And when she had finished she picked up her coat and left. As simple and as graceful as that.

That's what came back to me clearest of all.

Of One Mind

Sometimes I feel young and sometimes I feel old and sometimes I feel both at the same time. This trick of being in two minds, of weighing things on the one hand and then again on the other, has never been a problem for me. But, while I can hold two warring ideas in my head at any given moment, and even retain a clear idea of what it is I am thinking about, I am sometimes less sure of who or what it is that is doing the thinking. This weightlessness takes hold of me, this sense that somehow I am lacking essential ballast. I suspect it's one of the gifts of my generation, a generation becalmed in adolescence, a generation with nothing in its head or its heart and with too much time on its hands.

Lately, however, I'm experiencing something new and it has taken me a while to recognize it. Obscured behind amazement and something like awe, it has taken me weeks to see it clearly as the thing it really is. When I finally did get it straight in my mind I could hardly believe it.

To the best of my knowledge I have never experienced anything like it before, nor, living the type of life I've done, is there any reason why I should have. Take this example, an incident with my eight-year-old son only last week . . .

It was, on the face of it, a simple enough disappointment involving a school trip to an open farm outside the city. Giddy with anticipation, Jamie had talked about nothing else in the days leading up to it and, when I had met his questions with memories of my own upbringing on a small farm in west Mayo, his expectations had soared; the chance to see something of his dad's childhood promised to be a rare treat. But now the trip lay in ruins. Traffic congestion and a radio alarm clock flummoxed in the small hours by a power cut conspired to have us arrive at the school fifteen minutes after the bus had left. Now we stood in the stillness of his classroom, gazing at the neat rows of tables and seats, and I thought to myself that surely there was no place in all the world so full of absence as an empty classroom.

And Jamie's disappointment was huge. I had no need to look down at him to know it—I could feel it rolling off him, deep noxious waves of it. Just to have me in no doubt, he told me so himself.

"I'm disappointed," he said solemnly. "I can feel it here, right here." He placed his hand low on his chest and rubbed it up and down as if trying to relieve some digestive ache.

"Next week, Jamie," I assured him. "We can all go next week, the three of us. I promise."

"I'm in pain," he persisted. "Severe pain."

"You'll get over it," I replied shortly. "Next week, I said. Let's go."

I took him by the hand and led him out to the car. January light hung low in the sky, oppressive and tightening the muscles across my chest. I hated these winter months, the gloom that rose in my heart; summer seemed an infinity away.

"This isn't the first disappointment," Jamie said, as I held open the door for him. "They're beginning to mount up. I can feel the pressure."

"That bad?"

He nodded and sat in. "Yes, that bad. I'm only telling you for your own good."

"Be a man," I blurted. My own disappointment in letting him down now made me brusque. "And put on your seat belt."

There is, of course, no such thing as a simple disappointment, a small disappointment, to an eight-year-old. Fatherhood has taught me that feelings like these only come man-sized, brutally disproportionate to the cause, never calibrated to the dimensions of a child's world. They come with crushing intent, fully capable of annihilating their fragile universe. The wonder is that any child can survive even the slightest of them.

We drove back toward the city centre, the traffic loosened up now after the early rush hour. Jamie sat silently in the back seat. A glance in the rearview mirror showed him gazing out the side window, his moon-pale face pinched with the effort to hold back the tears.

He happened into my life over eight years ago, waking a dream of fatherhood that took me completely by surprise when it presented itself out of the blue some time before my thirtieth birthday. Before that, all my visions of children came with a completeness about them, which Jamie's arrival had totally confounded. Nothing in my idea of fatherhood had warned me about the fact that children do not drop fully formed out of the sky, nor of the ad hoc nature of fatherhood that is its day-to-day idiom; basically, nothing had warned me against screw-ups like this.

"Someday," he called suddenly from the back seat, leaving the word hanging in the air.

We had pulled into the first of the two roundabouts on the western edge of the city. Rain was falling, that resolute early-morning drizzle that tells you there will be no let-up for the day.

"Someday," he repeated, eying me in the rearview mirror.

"Someday what, Jamie? Speak up, don't be mumbling back there to yourself."

"Someday," he said, "when you're sitting in the visitors' gallery of the criminal court listening to the jury returning a guilty verdict on all charges and hearing the judge hand down the maximum sentence with no recommendation for bail, you will probably be asking yourself where did it all go wrong. Well, just to set your mind at rest, you need look no further than this morning."

"That bad?"

"I'm only telling you for your own peace of mind."

"Thank you, that's very kind of you. I'll remember that when I'm organizing your appeal."

Eight years ago I blundered out of my twenties, a feckless decade of drink and dope-smoking lived out against a soundtrack of white-boy guitar bands, a decade funded by various under-the-counter jobs and the most gullible welfare system in the western world. The setting up of the nation's second-language TV station drew me out, pallid and blinking into the light. Being fluent in

Irish scored me a contract subtitling the German and Scandinavian cartoons that bulked out the station's Irish-language quota in its early days. A month-by-month contract had opened out to a yearly one and all told I had now turned in seven of them. Each year I resolved to find something permanent and each year the relevant deadlines passed me by. This last year I had graduated from cartoons to captioning the station's twice-weekly soap opera, which now, in its fifth year, was responsible for a big percentage of the station's advertising revenue. A job that took me all of thirty hours a week left me with more than enough time with which to split parenting duties with Martha, Jamie's mother.

Back then the advent of a new TV station on the outskirts of this city had drawn a new type of female into the light. Upmarket and eager, all short skirts and high boots, they had a radiance that gave them allure in a city that till then had seen heavy boots and woolly sweaters as the uniform of bohemian aspiration and left-wing politics. And even if the majority of these new sirens were merely continuity announcers, weather girls and bit-part players in soaps, this did not diminish their glamour one bit; the city was grateful for the colour and open optimism they shed about them. This was Martha's milieu. She, too, had the looks and the stand-offish poise of a young woman with plenty of choices. Therefore, when I met her, it was somewhat gratifying to find that, in fact, her status was similar to my own. She, too, worked temporary contracts, honing scripts for continuity announcers and weather girls, all the time dreaming of an alternate life where she wrote code for video games, specifically strategic world-building games. At the time, she was working out the end of her current contract and thinking of moving to London where she hoped to find work in one of the many design studios that had sprung up after the launch of the PS2.

Six months after we met, a casual affair was brought to its senses by an unbroken blue line running through the window of a pregnancy test kit. Much solemn talking ensued, once more the old weighing of things against each other, only this time between two minds equally adroit at seeing both sides of any story without ever necessarily reaching a decision. Finally, however, we did rent a semi-D in one of the new estates on the city's outskirts and settled down to bringing up a child between us.

After three years we had to face up to the fact that we were hopelessly out of love. With the leaking away of all physical desire, our relationship bottomed out to a colourless haunting of each other, a leaching away of all feeling from our togetherness. We woke up to the conclusion that, were it not for the child between us, we would long ago have gone our separate ways. Some time in Jamie's third year we sat down and tallied up the cost of our lives together. All things considered, it hadn't been too expensive. One beloved child and the enrichment of sense and soul he had brought to us more than offset any regrets for dreams we had set aside on his account. Speaking for myself, it was the kind of balance sheet I could live with. We talked into the night, mapping out the details of an amicable separation, the terms of which would come into effect three years down the road when, we blithely reasoned, Jamie would be more of an age to cope with the trauma. We gave each other the love-you-but-not-in-love-with-you speech, agreed on the you-deserve-better postscript and then sat there ashamed of ourselves, quietly appalled that after three years and a child together this was the best we could do by way of a row. How could we have felt so little? Then, in a rush of gratitude toward each other, we made love for the first time in months. The following morning, embarrassed by such blundering intimacy, we renewed the vows of the night before.

When the three years were up, we sat Jamie down between us and told him that his family would now be divided between two houses. His reaction was muted, no hysterics or anxious pleading, no face-down pummelling of pillows. He walked into his room, pulled the door behind him and was not seen or heard of for the rest of that day. He came out later that evening and asked for something to eat, his face flushed, his whole being pulsing in a haze of anxiety.

A couple of weeks after that he began wetting the bed.

Lately he's got this idea, more accurately an obsession. How this idea has taken hold of him I cannot properly say but Martha dates it to the time of our break-up, the weeks and months after I moved out of our semi-D and into a two-bedroomed flat in the city centre. She speculates that it's all part of the break-up trauma, a childlike but nonetheless canny ploy with which to win treats and privileges off both of us. I listen to Martha because she is smarter than me and more attuned to the nuances of our child. Also, with her background in game programming, she is always likely to see chains of cause and effect.

But this time I have a feeling she's wrong. Jamie's conviction runs deeper than the circumstances of our break-up; it seems to come from the very depths of him, stirring something bleak in his young soul, filling him with words and ideas completely out of scale with his age.

One day he stepped into the kitchen draped in one of my old T-shirts and wearing a baseball cap back to front. His hands barely poked beyond the cuffs of the short sleeves and the baseball cap threatened to fall down over his eyes. It was a flashback to my grunge past, to a time at the beginning of the caring decade when, paradoxically, serial killers were valorized by a section of my generation as great counter-cultural heroes, heroic transgressors. The image leaped out in red ink, Michael Rooker in the title role, *Henry: Portrait of a Serial Killer.*

"Where did you get that?" I asked.

"The box."

"I thought I told you."

"Yeah, yeah—look at this." He held up the newspaper and tapped a headline in the middle of the page. "Kids Happy in War Games," it read.

"Tell me what it says. Sit down, this spaghetti is done."

He pulled out a chair and sat, spreading the paper out in front of him. "It says that children have become bored with swings and slides, too girly, they think, no thrills in them, no danger. Playgrounds are lying deserted all over Europe, no one using them. Then someone in Sweden had the idea of bringing in special-forces engineers to design these assault courses and now kids can't get enough of them."

I laid the plate on the table and handed him the fork and spoon. "Eat up. Those playgrounds will be closed down in a year. Health and safety, public liability, injuries and litigations, they'll be lucky to stay open."

Jamie shook his head. "That's where you're wrong. One broken elbow and a concussion—that's the injury list for twelve months in one of those playgrounds."

He folded up the newspaper, took off his cap and fell to eating. "What do you make of that, what does it mean?"

"Not with your mouth full." I handed him a napkin and he drew it across his mouth, streaking an orange blur halfway to his ears. "What would I know, kids are daft. Who knows what goes on in their heads?"

"That's true, look at me."

"Look at you indeed. Do you want to stay the night?"

"Yes."

"Finish your spaghetti and then call your mam."

"I already have."

A couple of weeks after we split up, Martha told me that Jamie had begun wetting the bed. Martha took him aside and asked him about it. If fear and disappointment come only in man-sized dimensions, so too does embarrassment. When it was mentioned to him, Jamie bolted from the kitchen and slammed the door on his bedroom. Martha bought a rubber sheet and told me not to say any more about it to him. A week later he brought the subject up himself.

"I need something," he said. "I'll come straight out with it."

"Yes."

"No beating around the bush or anything."

"I'm all ears."

"A request."

"Which is?"

"You won't like it."

"Jamie!"

"A beating."

"A what?"

"A beating."

He was framed in the doorway, a little study in misery. Once more he was the child wrestling with outsize miseries that threatened to engulf him.

"What have you done, Jamie? Whatever it is it can't be that bad."

"It's not what I've done, it's what I'm going to do."

"And what exactly are you going to do that warrants a beating?"

He pulled the chair out from the table and sat in. This is his way whenever he has something big to get off his chest. It seems to give him confidence, putting him in a position of strength, in so far as a child is ever in such a position. But just then he looked hesitant, teetering on the threshold of a great disclosure but unsure of how to begin.

"What is it you are going to do?" I persisted.

"I come from a broken home," he began.

"No, Jamie, you come from a home divided between two houses, you spend an equal time with each of us, whoever you want."

He shook his head, the flaw in the argument too obvious even to him. It was at times like this I had the feeling Jamie was streaking ahead of me, gaining on truths and ideas that by right I should have been handing down to him.

He spoke irritably. "By any definition of the normal family, I come from a broken home."

"Jamie, I'm only guessing but I don't think this is what you want to talk about."

"I wet the bed," he gasped desperately.

"Yes, I know, it's not a big thing, you'll get over it."

"I can't stop, each night I say my prayers and each morning I wake up covered in wee."

"God has a lot on his mind, Jamie. He's a busy man, you might have to wait your turn. But wetting the bed is no reason for a beating."

"I'm going to do something bad, something really bad."

"We all do something bad at one time or other. What is it you're going to do?"

"I'm going to kill someone."

"That is bad," I conceded. "Do you know who this someone is—it's not me, by any chance?"

He threw up his hands in a gesture of unknowing. "I don't

know," he said with some exasperation. "You'd want to take this seriously because you'll probably blame yourself later on and I wouldn't want that."

"How do you know you're going to kill someone?"

"There are signs," he said, "indications."

"This is that T-shirt. I told you before about going through my stuff."

"It's not the T-shirt," he yelled suddenly, "you're not listening."

I held up my hands. "Okay, I'm listening now. What signs?"

"Like I've said, I come from a broken home and I've started wetting the bed."

"And that's enough to turn you into a killer?" I felt distinctly odd discussing this with my eight-year-old son. Once more this sense of weightlessness came over me; I felt buoyant, unmoored from myself. From what I remembered, none of the parenting manuals Martha showed me had ever covered this kind of situation. However, I was certain also that I had to see this conversation through to the end. "What has this to do with wanting a beating?"

"The broken home and the bed-wetting are two of the classic signifiers of serial killers in their youth. The third one is parental abuse. In order to have a complete profile I need to have a beating. That is where you come in."

"Why would you want to kill anyone?"

"It is not that I want to kill anyone—it's just that that is the way it is going to be."

"This is ridiculous, Jamie. I'm sorry, there are no beatings here today."

He looked at me sadly and sighed. "You have a responsibility," he said softly. "Sooner or later the corpses will start turning up. Two with the same MO and signatures might be a coincidence, but three points to a serial killer. We have to give the investigation every chance. If we put a full profile in place now, that would put a halt to me before I get into my stride."

"This is nonsense, Jamie. This conversation is at an end." I got up from the table; he grabbed my wrist.

"He was quiet," he said fervently, "he kept to himself a lot." He fixed me with a glum stare. "That's what the neighbours will say when I'm being led away. Of course, long before that there will be all the other signs—the low self-esteem, the sexual inadequacies . . ." His voice trailed away.

"I'm sorry. There's no beatings here today. Or any other day, for that matter."

He raised his voice. "I'm only telling you, the child is the father of the man."

I talked to Martha about this the following day. She had finally moved her computer into the small box room I'd used as a work space when I'd lived there. A couple of personal items around the room claimed the space as her own. One of Picasso's blue women hung on the wall to her back and a series of little marble Buddhas stood ranked along the window sill, which looked down over the back garden. She knew nothing about Jamie's big idea.

"He hasn't mentioned anything to me about it. It sounds like a father and son thing."

"Does he spend much time on the Internet?"

"Only an hour or two each day, the laptop on the kitchen table where I can keep an eye on him. John, he's a good boy, I can't stop him doing everything his friends are doing at the moment. He has it tough enough as it is."

Every time she talks about Jamie I can see him in her face, the ghost of him flitting through her features: the same wide spacing of her eyes across her nose and the freckles on her forehead that stand out so vividly during these winter months. And it is already clear that if Jamie keeps growing at his present rate he is going to meet the same problems buying clothes as his mother—the narrow hips on which skirts and jeans drape sullenly and the skinny wrists that protrude beyond sleeves that are never long enough. It pleases me to see these shades of Martha in him; this continuance gladdens me. As for myself, while I take it for granted that there is indeed something of myself in my son, I can never quite put a finger on what this something is. If I press Martha on the subject, she tells me airily that we are both the same age.

"This worries me, Martha. You should have heard him, all these technical terms and a rationale as well. And this beating thing . . ."

"Did you give it to him?"

"No, Jesus!"

She grinned openly. "I know, I'm winding you up, you're so easy. Listen, he's a smart kid, everyone says so. And he's probably sneaked a handful of *CSI* episodes or *Criminal Minds*—but that's all, he's a healthy and happy kid with an imagination he's still trying on for size. Everything will be okay."

"Let's talk to him together, this has me really spooked."

She pivoted from the chair and kissed me on the cheek. Over her shoulder her computer screen was frozen; in the middle of a rolling landscape two tiny figures were arrested in their flight toward a dark forest.

"Leave it to me," she said, "it might need a mother's touch. But I'm telling you, I'm not going to be guilt-tripped on this. We're good parents and he's not the first kid to have a bed-wetting thing."

"Just do what you can, have a word." I nodded to the screen. "What game is it this time?"

She waved a narrow wrist.

"*Orcland.* A centuries-long dispute between elves and orcs, border violations, rustling, water rights, mineral rights, it goes back to the dawn of time. I have to tip the balance of power toward the elves, upgrade their armour and ordnance. Market research has shown that elves' approval rating has risen across all demographics. The gaming community has reacted badly to seeing them getting their arses kicked so easily. I have to even the odds a little for the new add-on."

"They're still not going to win, the template is fixed."

"I know, I can only help them make a better fight of it. Well, fairer at least."

"What sort of job is that for a grown woman?" I teased.

"The type of job that pays the rent and puts food on the table."

I sat on her chair and gazed at the screen. Two elves were streaking toward a great forest where they would find refuge and a cache of arms. Somewhere off-screen they were no doubt being pursued by a posse of murderous orcs. Tipping the balance of power, tilting the odds toward the elves; this is the type of thing Martha did.

"Martha, how did we get to be this trivial, elves and subtitles? How did we ever get sidetracked into this shite?"

She shrugged, shook her head. "Don't ask me. But you show me another job that comes up with food and rent at twenty hours a week and I'll consider it. Till then I've got elves to arm." She giggled suddenly, put her hand on my shoulder. "John," she said, "don't worry, his name is Jamie, not Damien."

"Not funny, Martha."

"Sorry, it was too juicy, I couldn't sidestep it."

Whatever way she broached the subject, she made no headway with Jamie. And whatever he said to her in reply left her in no doubt that this was something between men. No, there was no drawing him out on the subject—he'd talk it out with Dad, he said. So I left him to it, hoping he might put the whole thing behind him, thinking that if he needed to talk about it badly enough he would bring the subject up in his own good time. And sure enough he did. We were sitting together on the couch after a double episode of *The Simpsons*.

"You haven't given my request any more thought?"

"No, I can't say I have, how about you?"

He squirmed round to face me, tucking his feet in under him.

"Yes, I have it all figured out. Yesterday I killed a spider, I wrote it into my diary—that covers the cruelty to animals part. One beating now and I will have a complete profile, the homicidal triad, every box ticked off. Any investigation would have to be blind not to be able to track me down. But I need that beating. One beating registered with the childcare authorities and the job will be complete." He rolled up his sleeves, revealing his skinny upper arms. "You could confine your work to areas of soft tissue, my thighs and arms, places where the bruising will be obvious but not dangerous. But nothing around the head, you don't want to risk a charge of attempted homicide."

"And how's that going to make me look, a registered child beater?"

"I'll clear your name. I'll say it was totally out of character, I pushed you to the end of your tether."

"You're a serial killer, who's going to believe you?"

"I'm under oath, I won't lie."

"And I thought there was something in those profiles about fire-starting."

"I could fix that easily enough."

"Don't bother. And this profile thing, it's an American template."

"So?"

"It might not translate across the Atlantic."

He shook his head sadly. "Dad, the world is of one mind. That's the way it is."

"It doesn't have to be like that. These things aren't fixed."

I put my arm round him and drew him into my side. There wasn't a pick on him, his body a soft assemblage of angles, all elbows and shoulder blades. "How do you know these things, Jamie, where do you get these ideas from?"

"How does anyone know anything? I just pick them up along the way, same as anyone; this is all common knowledge."

"It's not common to me. Why don't you turn yourself in now, before you do any damage?"

"Who would believe an eight-year-old?" He turned his face up to me. "Would it kill you?"

"I'll never know."

He lowered his face. "I'm only for your good," he said, "you'll thank me for this later on."

I sat there long after he'd gone to bed, the TV on mute.

Someone told me that you know nothing of love till you have a child of your own. You know nothing of its unconditional demands nor the things you might do to protect it. And this is what I've been feeling these last few weeks, this is what spooks me. I've seen enough to know that wherever there is love there are opportunities for guilt. It has something to do with more laws and prohibitions, more opportunities for misdeeds and transgressions.

What spooks me now is that Jamie's fear will become my fear, his terror my terror. I worry that one day it might spread from him, slip through his narrow boundaries and become mine. That old sense of weightlessness comes over me as I think these things; once more I am at a remove, standing at arm's length from myself ... And one night, at the end of my tether, the world really might be of one mind. And because I haven't the courage to be scared, the courage to take up the full duty of love, I might find myself pitched into a place beyond marvelling that I could ever go this far. And because this is the age of reasoned hysterics and because I am haunted by his pale arms, I might find myself walking down the hall to his bedroom. And sitting on the side of his bed, lit by the light streaming in from the hall, I would run through my reasons once more, squaring my story against the day when I will stand up and tell the truth, the whole truth and nothing but the truth. And then, these things straight in my head at last, I will reach out to touch his shoulder, touch him gently, calling his name in a whisper that barely reaches into his sleep ... "Jamie, wake up, Jamie, wake up, good boy ..."

And that I can think these things and see them so clearly, that for a few moments I am so completely lost to myself ...

Heaven's Mandate

You will not recognize him now.

Forget every memory you have of him, all those images in photo and newsprint that captured him in all his young promise as the coming man, the great white hope, when he strode onto the national stage. Forget the handsome face atop the long neck and the haughty carriage that lent him that irrefutable air of Providence. Forget also the declamatory style, that tone of airy certainty in which so many of us put our faith. Forget all these things and summon instead every cliché of decline and set them against the man who once topped six foot four inches and who drew the eye so easily in all those Cabinet photographs in which he loomed, head and shoulders above his colleagues. Gaze instead upon this terrible decline, the coda of a cautionary tale wound on beyond its final pages.

This room is not what we would have expected. The walls are

papered with old campaign posters, some curling at the bottom, some threatening to lift away at the corners and tear through the diagonals. All of them carry his photograph, and the earliest ones date back to his first campaign in the late seventies. Beneath these icons of his younger self he now sits in a wingback chair, looking out the window and down over the lawn to the seashore. At this moment his view is blocked by the woman standing with her back to him. She is broad-shouldered and planted solidly on the ground and we can infer from her flat shoes and her one-piece uniform that she is here in some official capacity—most likely representing one of the caring professions. Her name is Catherine and we know this from the name tag pinned on her right breast.

"No one can tell me it was not beautiful," he says suddenly, swiping the air with a feeble hand. "No one."

"Yes," she says, turning from the window, "no one can tell you it was not beautiful."

She reserves a special tone for him when he's in this mood, a dull, placatory register that lies almost beneath hearing; it's as if she needs him to lean close so she can be assured he is fully attentive.

"Once more, Catherine, my first day in office . . ."

We notice now that he no longer speaks of himself in the third person. That regal idiom, which made him such a soft target for satirists and which too often occluded his real gifts, has given way to the full intimacy of the first person.

"My first day, Catherine," he persists, "my first day."

She turns from the window—there is nothing out there for her.

"It was a glorious day," she begins, "the elements themselves deferred to the occasion; the sun recused itself from the sky. At any moment the clouds might have parted to give God a clearer view."

"They were affected, the elements?"

"Yes, they were affected."

She would welcome an interruption now, any sort of interruption. Someone with a questionnaire, for instance. She has heard they are out there, people with questionnaires traipsing the land on various need-to-know assignments. A few questions about her marital status, her number of dependents, her religious affiliation, if any . . . she would gladly answer a few of those queries right now. Anything would be better than this.

"And how did I present myself on that first day?"

"You wore a white suit."

"And that was unusual?"

"Oh yes."

"What was the word?"

"Transfigured."

"Yes! And there was no precedent for that?"

"No, no one had ever seen the like."

"Ha!" He clapped his hands smartly. "Of course not, I was always a step ahead. And what did I say, the clincher, who did I quote?"

"You quoted Isaiah."

"Of course, the prophet." He sighs fondly at the memory and shakes his head. "I agonized over that, I won't deny it. Would it be lost on them, would it go over their heads?" He throws up his hands. "Of course it went over their heads. I scanned the editorials the following day and of course they missed it. But they remember it now." He falls silent, his chin dipping into his chest, one hand cupping the other. She has noticed this new habit lately—his left thumb in the palm of his right hand and this continual twisting action that threatens to torque it out at the root. She has noticed how it becomes particularly vengeful during these pauses in his story. On resumption he will stop, overcome with that irresistible brightening that always brings him back to himself. As if on cue . . .

"And what did I say?"

"You said that the Messiah would come out of the west."

"I did indeed. That's exactly what I said. And did I lie?"

"No, you were as good as your word."

"Yes."

She turns to the window once more. But even with her back to him, she can sense his tongue flicking over his cracked lips, this anxious tic preparatory to the final push. She can anticipate him now but she prefers to let him have his say. One of his peevish fits is the last thing she needs at this moment.

"And how did I do it, Catherine, how did I fulfil my mission?"

Not for the first time something mean in her wants to toy with him, something bitter in her wanting recompense for all the hours she has spent in this room with him. But she dare not risk it; there is something uncanny about him when he is in these moods.

"Catherine!"

"Yes?"

"My mission."

She turns and sees him looking expectantly at her. Lowering her eyes, she begins in a dull singsong.

"You came to restore time and you did it by building roads and bridges and bypasses."

"Yes," he breathes, "roads and bridges and bypasses. And there was a formula?"

"Yes. An average of three thousand cars a day with one point four occupants in every one . . . each vehicle spending seventeen minutes in traffic jams . . . multiply one by the other and divide by twenty-four and you get one thousand, one hundred and ninety hours . . . do the same sum with the alternate five-minute journey through the roundabout, take one from the other and you get eight hundred and forty hours."

"Eight hundred and forty hours," he intones solemnly, "restored to the living."

"Multiplied by the number of working days in a year and . . ."

"Stop," he cries happily, "my head . . ."

He succumbs to a weak giggle and passes his hand across his face. After a moment he waves her on. "Cut to the chase, the sum total."

"According to the World Health Organization, at year's end the sum total of thirty-five men's lives."

The figure leaves him stunned, as though he is hearing it for the first time and not, as is the case, rehearsing it for the umpteenth. His face tightens to a grimace of satisfaction.

"This is what I did, thirty-five men per annum restored to the living. And over my lifetime?"

"Multiply by . . ."

He silences her once more with a weak stamp of a slippered foot. For all his love of hearing this, he has only ever had a limited degree of patience. And it is always likely to give way to awe.

"It beggars belief. That one man . . ." He tails off, the sentence drooping in the bright air. "And if I did not raise the dead themselves, it was only a matter of time; sooner or later they would be elbowing their way up out of their graves."

She turns back to the window. If past form is anything to go by, this is where he will lapse into silence, his anger and inspiration finally spent. Outside, the tide is at the low water mark, ready to turn at any moment. She readies herself, trying to attune her mind to this short interval when the sea is neither ebbing nor flowing. It is a game she plays with herself, something in her is comforted by this short period of stillness and balance.

"Catherine."

"Yes?"

"Did they not weep with gratitude?"

She turns once more. His eyes glisten. She remains silent. He does not flinch from her gaze.

"This will soon be over and I will not be sorry," he says.

Now he shrugs himself up in the chair, squares his shoulders and plants both feet bluntly on the floor. Rallying himself, that's what he's doing. He wags a finger at her. "Someday soon I will be standing on the floor of heaven and I will be asked to account for myself. And this is what I will point to—thirty-five men per annum restored to their lives, my life's work. No wonder my health is broken, no wonder my . . . and I will point to the electoral register and say, *This is my mandate, this is my authority: thirty-three percent of the total valid poll, each time returned with a bigger margin than the last; roundabouts and bypasses, bridges and dual carriageways . . .* These are the things I did, Catherine, these are the things I will point to. And then I will say, *Now show me your mandate, you prick . . . you etiolated cunt.*"

The savagery of the curse startles him, the sudden force of it driving him back into the chair. But he concludes in a loud, desperate bark, "These are the words I will use, Catherine, the very words."

Despite herself she is impressed; he has never pushed it this far before, never to this end. But in truth she is already bored. The day is gone when she would have found herself caught up in the story, drawn in by his enthusiasm and sometimes moved to embellish it with colour and detail all her own. It has been a while since such flights of fancy took hold of her. Now she stands looking out the window, down over the green lawn to where it ends on the jagged line of the seashore. She has a life of her own outside of this room, she must have, there is surely something out there waiting for her. But for the moment there is nothing but a vacant listlessness within her.

Even with her back turned to him she can sense the grinding effort it has taken him to push this far. His exhaustion fills the room like interference. She knows what it will cost him . . . the long night of fevered sleeplessness ahead, his bedding twisted into damp ropes.

Behind her, in his chair, he turns out the palms of his hands and looks imploringly at her back.

"And they carried me shoulder-high, Catherine," he whispers hoarsely, "they carried me shoulder-high."

Forensic Songs

Every time he enters a crime scene he experiences the moment as an absolute transition, as if he is crossing into a different realm. The crime scene is the frozen world; circumstances have run to their conclusion here and time has taken itself elsewhere.

The detective's attention is drawn to the wound on her left temple. He studies the angle and depth of it and gazes up at the spray of blood that fans out across that part of the wall near where she must have stood. So telling are these details that he is already pre-empting the pathologist's report: *She was struck from behind with a blunt instrument; at the last moment she turned round, turned her head into the blow.* On the other side of the corpse, the pathologist ducks out under the tape. Without a word of greeting, the detective calls to him.

"Do we have a time of death?"

The pathologist pulls the hood back from his lab suit and fixes his gaze in the middle distance. "I have to do a full examination but based on lividity and rigor mortis I would say the corpse is about twenty-four hours old, certainly not a lot more."

The pathologist leaves the room and the detective steps aside to let the crime-scene photographer circle the corpse a final time. Now he turns his attention to the room itself. The large table in the middle of the floor is littered with open journals and copy-books, reference books and a small ashtray with a few butts in the bottom. Among the journals is a wallet. It contains a couple of credit cards, a library photo pass and a couple of twenties. Nothing else, no photos of loved ones, no receipts, no address. He looks up and sees his new assistant detective across the table from him. He hands the wallet to her.

"Detective Kennedy."

"Kenny, sir."

"Kenny, yes. There's a name, a few other bits and pieces here, see what you can find," he says and then turns out of the room into the daylight where time and circumstance pick up the run of themselves once more.

"Here."

The man hands his wife a mug of tea and sits apart from her at the other end of the sofa. It is a large sitting room dominated across its centre by the sofa, which faces the fireplace and the flat-screen TV. The room is lit from the rear by two up-lighters that cast down a soft glow. Over the fireplace there is a fine line drawing of a child in three-quarter pose, a sensitively realized piece that shows real talent on the part of the draughtsperson. The man stretches out on the sofa, his whole body and posture asserting his right to slob out in his own house at the end of a day's work.

"So what's happened?" he asks.

"It's just begun," his wife says. "The detective has been called to a crime scene. A young woman is found in a rented house lying face down with her head bashed in. There is blood on the walls but no sign of a struggle."

She is sitting with her bare feet tucked up under her and in spite of the late hour there is an energy and alertness about her that gives the impression she still has work to do. Her dark hair is pulled back in a girlish headband, which gives full exposure to a face that is clearly in its late thirties but has yet to show any signs of droop or sag. And if she is too plain to be anyone's idea of beauty, it is easy to see that most men will eventually confess to being attracted to her without being able to say why.

"And these are the crime-scene photos?"

"Yes."

The detective spreads a series of photos across his desk. From various angles they show the young woman lying face down on the timber floor, her head haloed in a pool of blood. The picture sequence glances over the deep wound on her left temple, the blood on the wall over where she stood, and ends finally in a couple of wide-angle scenes of the room itself. She is lying between the table and the wall, her head near the skirting board. Using her body to establish scale, it is easy to calculate the size of the room as something like fifteen feet by twelve. A large table in the middle of the room is scattered with books and open writing pads; a couch stands against one wall and the others are decorated with cheap prints of old masters in generic frames. The last photo shows a single window opening onto a large beach over which a high summer sun shines.

The detective has a theory about corpses, specifically murder victims. His theory has it that all murder victims are ashamed; all are acutely aware of themselves as a blemish on creation, a despoiling of the natural order. They feel this deeply and they protest that they are not merely this brutal set of circumstances, this shambles lying here on the floor. At the moment of death they make one last flailing attempt to establish their death within the widest laws of the universe. This is their last despairing act of faith in the world because the dead, no more than the living, cannot abide chaos and will not lie in eternity without making peace with the world . . .

No, he has never voiced this theory to anyone and he is unsure what part of himself is responsible for it. All he knows is that he can never look at photographs like these without thinking of it. He shuffles through the photos and stops on a close-up of her skull. He studies the angle of the wound and by shifting the photographs he lines it up with the spray pattern on the wall above her. Now it is clear that she had to have been struck by someone who was left-handed. That narrows it down. Is this what he is looking for?

With nothing more to be gleaned from them, the detective squares the photos into a file. A mortuary technician leans into his office.

"We have a time of death—close to the original guesstimate, she died sometime in the middle of Sunday afternoon."

"Any other wounds?"

"None, no impact marks, no ligatures, no sign of sexual assault."

"Just the single blow."

The detective turns his gaze back to the file on the desk. The camera pans back from him and in this uncertain mood the scene freezes and fades to a title screen; cue the first ad break.

• • •

The woman on the sofa takes up the remote and turns the sound down. She turns to her husband.

"So," she says abruptly, "what's your alibi, mister?"

"What?"

"Your alibi, you're dragged in for questioning on this."

The man does not have to think—he sees instantly what's afoot. They are both fans of these late-night cop shows and sometimes they have this game of second-guessing the plots with the sound turned off. It's a game they have played several times for their own enjoyment. There are no winners or losers, just the shared satisfaction of building a coherent story that covers the facts and the circumstances; a convincing account they can both agree on with as few holes and contradictions as possible.

But tonight the man is not in the mood. He groans deeply; he's had a long day and he's bone-tired. But one look at his wife's vivid expression and he sees immediately that she will not be thwarted. He will have to ease himself into it; he decides to begin by playing for time.

"Why am I dragged in for questioning?"

"You've been seen with her. This is a small town, people have seen you buying drinks and flirting with her."

"I'm a suspect?"

"You're the only one."

"What would I want with her? I'm a married man with two kids."

The woman shakes her head with a pitying expression; apparently this protest is so naïve it barely warrants further comment.

"Look at her," she urges, "her looks, the sexy summer dress, the rented house—this is exactly the sort of woman a married man might have a fling with. A couple of months screwing her over the summer and when September comes she will have gone back to where she came from. You'd better have a pretty secure alibi because right now you're the only suspect."

Early as it is in the game, he sees that there is something especially forceful about her tonight, something pointedly relentless and aggressive.

She is looking at him without blinking. This is a more forceful and sudden challenge than he is used to. The sequence of photographs flashes through his mind.

"Okay," he relents, "as it happens I do have an alibi, a secure one with witnesses."

"Good, let's hear it."

"Time of death was established as twenty-four hours before the corpse was found, right?"

"Yes."

"Let's say twenty-four hours ago was the afternoon of Sunday twenty-seventh."

"Okay."

"Well, in the middle of Sunday afternoon, almost exactly at the TOD, I was thirty miles away, lining out at wing forward for our club in the first game of the championship. In the twentieth minute I got yellow-carded and my name was entered into the ref's notebook; in the fifty-eighth minute I scored an equalizing point and that, too, was recorded by the ref and witnessed by the whole team and no less than a hundred spectators. Furthermore, later that week, the local paper carried a photo of me jumping for a ball in that same game. So, all these things, eyewitness reports, referee's game report and photos place me at least thirty miles away at the time of her death. I couldn't have done it."

The man sits back. He has surprised himself with this sudden inspiration; he has seldom been this sharp. Now he considers; if there is a flaw in his reasoning it is not immediately obvious. The woman nods appreciatively.

"That's good," she concedes.

"It's better than good, it's waterproof. You have to let me go."

"Maybe. It remains to be seen how your alibi holds up when we begin to examine it."

"What do you mean, 'when we begin to examine it'? There is no flaw in it as far as I can see. You keep holding onto me and I will bring a case of unlawful detention."

"We'll see."

She picks up the remote once more and points it at the TV.

Detective Kenny enters his office. She is new and eager and she has that bright appearance of someone who is used to bringing good news. Now she pauses inside the door with what may be a dramatic sense of her new role, or may be something more diffident. Either way he lets her stand there, framed from behind in the blue light; whatever the moment he has no wish to spoil it for her.

"We have an ID," she eventually blurts.

"Yes."

"The cards in her wallet tell us that her name is Alice Rynne. She was twenty-five and she worked as a counsellor for the Irish Adoption Authority. For the last three months she had been on sabbatical while she completed a course of study—she was doing a postgrad diploma through the Open University. She rented the house from a family friend and was staying there while she wrote up her thesis. Her topic was on attachment disorders in Romanian adoptees. The theme has special resonance for her— she herself was adopted from an orphanage in Arad in western Romania when she was two years old. She had been living in that house for the last two months."

"Did she have any callers, friends or boyfriends?"

"We're checking that at the moment."

"This is a small town, a single woman with her looks would have drawn attention. Let me know when you have something else."

She leaves the office and the detective watches her go.

The woman turns to her husband and looks at him expectantly. In moments like this he has the uneasy feeling that he is not wholly himself but more exactly the willed object of her imagination, something she has drawn up out of thin air. It has often crossed his mind that he is nothing more than her imaginary friend, something she constructed long ago in the bored afternoon of a gifted childhood. He also feels himself to be attention dependent—without her gaze he might flicker and fade away entirely. But right now he feels totally invoked and compelled to participate in her game. Whatever her childhood pastimes, her games are more complex now, the rules and objectives knotted in ways he can barely guess at. Having no choice, he decides to enter the game immediately.

"So I'm having an affair with this woman."

"Yes."

"I'm a married man with two kids."

"I didn't say you weren't."

"But . . ."

"That's why they're called affairs."

"Let me guess—my wife and kids have driven me into the arms of this woman."

"Yes."

"Why?"

"You have disappointments, grievances."

"Do I?"

"Yes."

"You might as well spell them out."

"Okay, these are the facts. You are a small-town man so you have small-town grievances—the wife and kids you lumbered yourself with in your early twenties and the football career which suffered as a result; all the travel you never got around to; screwing the same woman your whole life; the aging mother left on your hands by a brother and sister who took off when they saw the writing on the wall; all these things."

"That's some list."

"Yes, it is. There is no single item on it capable of driving you into the arms of another woman but all of them together and targeted at that raw spot ... well, this is the kind of bitterness you succumb to in a small place like this."

"There's a big gap between being pissed off and being a killer."

"Yes, admittedly motive is a bit blurred at the moment."

"And with no motive you have no case?"

"The investigation is ongoing."

She turns her attention back to the television. On screen the assistant detective has entered a local pub. The place is quiet—four or five men along the counter supping their pints. The barman stands with his back to the shelves, his arms folded across his chest. Detective Kenny takes her drink to a table by the back wall and listens to the hum of conversation. Talk goes up and down the bar.

"... riding her ..."

"... so I believe ..."

"... no ..."

"... yes ..."

"... lot of talk ..."

"... *dúirt bean liom* ..."

"... always be talk ..."

"... lads putting legs under it ..."

"... I'm only saying ..."

"... put it past him, though ..."

"... always fond of it, the same boyo ..."

"... the wren's nest ..."

"... yes ..."

"... in fairness ..."

"... aren't we all, if we could get it ..."

"... unless he's changed ..."

"... and changed in a big way ..."

"... I don't know ..."

"... lads doing more talking than riding ..."

"... talking ..."

"... sympathy for him ..."

The assistant detective stands in the doorway and coughs. It is clear that she is still finding her way in this new environment. As yet she is not wholly sure of her cues and entrances. She waits for the detective to raise his head.

"She was having an affair," she says simply.

"Who was having an affair?"

"Alice Rynne."

"You've asked around?"

"Yes. As you've said, this is a small town; she was seen flirting with a man and there is definite word that she was having a thing with this person."

"He's local?"

"Yes, forty years old, married with two kids."

For the first time he notices that she has a gap between her two front teeth, a gap that seems to take its cue from the severe centre parting that runs through her hair. He remembers reading somewhere that in some cultures this signifies a certain type of sensual promise; he makes a note to himself that he must stop watching the Discovery Channel. Her CV mentioned that she has training in ballistics but beyond that he does not know much about her. She has shown real eagerness and efficiency in this investigation so far, but there has also been a degree of impatience with the slow progress. He has yet to decide if this is a newcomer's proper anxiety to impress or whether it is indicative of something more headstrong. Time will tell.

"Will we bring him in for questioning?" she asks.

He shakes his head. "Not just yet, it's too soon and we don't have enough on him. Believe me, if we go hauling in every married man in the village who bought her a drink we would have the place full in no time. No, go to his house, show your face and ask him a few questions; let him know how much you know and see how he reacts."

She nods, turns on her heel and is gone.

"So what would you say to her?" the woman asks. "Suppose the doorbell was to go at this moment and she was there on your doorstep, flashing her badge, wanting to question you. How would you react?"

"How do you think I'd react? I'd just give her my alibi and that would be it, game over."

"So you're wagering all on this alibi of yours?"

"Why not?"

"I don't buy it," she says softly. "It's too anxious."

She sweeps the remote through the air and kills the sound on the TV. Now he senses that she is about to pounce—all her energies and pulses seem barely contained within her.

"What's too anxious?"

"Your alibi."

"I was playing football, what's anxious about that?"

"That's not what you said."

"I said I was playing football."

The woman shakes her head and looks into the distance. "No, you didn't. The exact phrase you used was 'lining out at wing forward.' I took note of it."

"So? That's what footballers do, they line out. You're clutching at straws." He stifles an urge to throw up his hands in exasperation. "This is going nowhere."

"Think about it, it's ridiculous. You're forty years of age, three stone over your fighting weight, what makes you think you can still get a game at wing forward?"

"I was a good footballer, skill doesn't leave you."

"Skill no, but speed yes. You can't tell me that at your age you're still getting a game on the wing. You may have the skill but you do not have the legs for it. In fact, the foul you got carded for was for pulling and dragging—that's exactly the type of foul that someone whose speed has deserted them would be pulled for. Your alibi is at least questionable on one point."

"That's a small point."

"I reckon the only way you are going to get a game in the championship at your age is on a scrappy junior B team: stick you in at full forward where you won't have to do any running."

It takes him a moment to acknowledge that he will have to concede this further point. "Okay, I was playing junior B, another minor detail."

"Not so minor at all."

"It does not disprove what the ref and the spectators saw."

"Yes, the spectators—about a hundred, you said."

"About that, give or take."

"Only a hundred spectators at a championship game on a summer Sunday?"

"The first game of the championship, it was a slow start."

"My guess is that it wasn't a Sunday. Summer Sundays are not clogged up with scrappy junior B games. Junior B matches are played on weekday evenings or on Saturdays. Either of those makes it possible that you were at the crime scene around the time of her death. That alibi of yours is full of holes."

She is exaggerating but there is no denying she has bent his story out of shape. He is not fully exposed but he does need to rethink his position. She moves off the sofa toward the door and calls back over her shoulder.

"If I was you I'd start getting a lawyer, mister."

She walks up the gravel drive to the house and stands on the doorstep, pressing the bell. Waiting for the door to open, she steps back on the concrete walk and surveys the front of the house. It's an ordinary hip-roof house on the outskirts of the village, one of several such along both sides of the main road. But little details distinguish it; there is a degree of taste and wealth evident in the pea gravel and lawn lamps that set the house apart from its neighbours. The battered tradesman's van in the drive gives an improbable hint as to where this wealth might have come from. Now the door opens and a man stands there in his shirtsleeves and socks.

"John Crayn?"

"Yes."

"I'm Detective Kenny. I was wondering if I could ask you a few questions."

"Questions about what?"

"About the death of Alice Rynne."

She sees him check something within him, some pulse running ahead of itself. She's not sure what to make of it. She has radar but does not always know how to interpret the signals it receives. It could mean anything, innocent surprise or an anxious man putting his guard up.

"I don't know anything about her death."

"We have reason to believe you knew her."

"I'm not answering any more questions." As he makes to close the door, she raises her voice.

"It would be better if we did this now, Mr. Crayn. The alternative is that I bring you into the station and hold you overnight. I suggest you answer a few questions and get it over with."

Crayn looks her up and down and scans the road behind her. Then he stands back and motions her inside. She steps past him into the hallway and then turns into the sitting room; he leaves the door open to follow her.

"I thought you people came in pairs," he says. "I didn't think they sent anyone on their own."

"We're only having a conversation; why would I need to be chaperoned?"

"It's just that on the telly . . . suit yourself."

"Are you alone, Mr. Crayn?"

"Yes, my wife is at work."

"Where does she work?"

"She works in Allergan, a pharmaceutical company; she's a HR manager."

"And your kids, you have a boy and a girl?"

"They're in their teens, they don't tell me where they go."

He looks bigger amid the comfortable furniture of the sitting room; his chest has now broadened out to its full width and his shoulders swell through his heavy work shirt. He smells of cement and his face has the pinched creases of a man who has suffered long exposure to its heat and dry burn. And although he is only forty there is no trace whatsoever of the young man he recently was. The face, all that compacted muscle—had she not known she would have said he was ten years older. It is clear he wants her gone so he pushes straight to the point.

"Yes, I heard about her death but I know nothing about it."

"We have witnesses who say that you were very friendly with her."

"I'm friendly with a lot of people."

"I was thinking more than friendly."

He shakes his head. "I bought her a drink, I flirted with her. There was nothing more to it than that." He draws himself up to his full height.

"Did you ever leave her home after closing time?"

"No, never."

"I find that hard to believe. You spend the evening talking and flirting and buying her drink and you never offered to drive her home?"

"I might have offered but she did not take it up."

"You're saying you were never in her house?"

"I'm saying I'm a married man with two kids. I take all that seriously, Detective. Now is there anything else?"

"One last thing; where were you on the afternoon of the twenty-seventh?"

"The twenty-seventh was what, Sunday, Monday?"

"Sunday."

"If it was Sunday I was playing football."

"You have witnesses?"

"Yes, how many do you need?"

His rigid stance is his way of telling her that her work in this room is finished.

. . .

He raises his hand before she can speak. It's not his way to cut across his wife like this but he has an anxious need that he does not rightly understand; a need to establish something.

"Okay," he says with as narrow an emphasis as he can manage. "It's easy to see where this is going. Let's turn to the question of what's happening between the two people who have an involvement with this woman. Let's turn to their marriage. The detective has just learned that this man's wife is a corporate career woman; she heads up a HR division. We can see the conclusions she will draw from that. She will wager that the relative social positions within their marriage have created an imbalance of some sort, a kind of shamed tension in the man which comes to a head and spills over into violence, ending up with this young woman lying face down in a pool of her own blood. Is that an accurate summary?"

"Yes, that would be my read on it, pretty accurate."

He makes no effort to hide his disgust. "Well, it may be accurate, but it's also tiresome, hackneyed. It's the old story, some tired drama of a midlife crisis which ends in bloodshed. Some idiot who can't manage his grievances, or keep them to himself; life has disappointed him so now someone has to pay. Boohoohoo, fuck him."

He is surprised by the rising register of his voice, it seems to have snagged on some rage within himself, drawing it up from a hollow place.

She is looking at him carefully. "I think that's one telling of it, but as to how that version ends in this dead woman—I'm not so sure about that. How about this version: the story of a man usurped from within himself. Once upon a time a young man set aside certain dreams and freedoms for a wife and family. He set aside the drink and the screwing and the travel and even the football career he might have had for a life with a wife and kids. He turns his back on Jack-the-lad and settles for being a good husband and a good father. The years go by, a family is raised and one day he looks up and sees that his youth is way behind him, fading fast in his rearview mirror . . ."

"And that comes as news to him?"

"No, not at all, that doesn't come as news to him, but his own reaction to it does. He feels cheated, aggrieved, overwhelmed by a feeling of something lost. He tries to tell himself that it's okay, he's raised two happy, healthy kids, he has a nice house and he's comfortable—he's not wealthy by any means but neither he nor his family want for anything. And he realizes that this is what he has gambled on as a young man and he sees now that he has won—all these things are his—wife, kids, house and money, the whole lot. He has it solved. And yet . . . and yet there's this voice inside him, a voice he has never heard before, a little shrill voice screaming at him, saying, 'No, fuck it, none of this is enough, this is a shit deal, I've been swindled; fuck the house and the kids, fuck the wife and the money—what's in it for me, what do I get?'"

The man snorts derisively. "You can't expect sympathy for that fucker, he needs to stop pissing and moaning and get some balls."

"And that's the point. Life wasn't happy taking his youth, it had to take his balls, too. As the detective pointed out, the woman he married thrived; she has gone on to a high-flying career heading up a human resources division—that's a lot more than he's done. While she's attending seminars in behavioural psychology, he is out with his hawk and trowel, covered in cement. It's not hard to guess which side of the house the prestige is on."

"And he can't find it in himself to be happy or proud of her?"

"He would like to, he's not a bad man, but there's that little voice inside him protesting, giving him no peace. On and on it goes . . . he's not proud of how he feels but that voice won't give him any rest."

"So why come up with that alibi?"

She groans in dismay. "Are we back to that again?"

"Yes."

"There's no serious flaw in it but there is just enough anxious vanity with which to twist it out of shape. And this same vanity might accommodate the type of violence we have here."

"Bollocks!"

"No, just think—this man feels he owes it to himself, one last fling before it is too late, before he gets too fat and too old. Remember the photos; remember how she looked—that hair, those legs. Remember that she flirted with him, the conversations she had with him and the drinks he bought her—a couple of months' remorseless fucking and he might be able to call it quits, shut the voice up in your head once and for all. Square it with your conscience. You might feel you owe yourself that. Remember, you haven't just come to fuck her, you've come to collect."

"I?"

"I, you, whoever."

He has the sudden sense of himself falling, something in him coming unhinged and spilling over an edge. The sensation is all the more frightening in that he is fully aware of himself sitting on the sofa. But this is what she loves. For all the forensic truth-seeking in traces and wavelengths, she knows that the real truths are found in the raw ground of the human heart, that fevered realm. Now she has the scent of blood in her nostrils and he can sense her savage relish. This focused aggression is heedless to the damage it might cause, the things said that cannot be taken back, the wounds old and new, caused and reopened . . . She is ready to push on and risk everything and he realizes that for as long as he can remember he has been afraid of this woman, not merely for what she is capable of doing but for who she is, this woman, his wife . . .

The stillness of her pose tells him that she is fully aware of him looking at her. She raises her chin as if sitting for her portrait.

On screen, Detective Kenny has visited the local pub again. Once more she takes her drink to the back wall and listens.

"... a couple of times, out the back smoking ..."

"... blonde hair and ..."

"... fine-looking ..."

"... early twenties ..."

"... I'd have said older ..."

"... I won't argue, you're a good judge ..."

"... wife of his ..."

"... where they met ..."

"... the back smoking ..."

"... talk away and have the craic with you ..."

"... lovely ..."

"... student, I think ..."

"... Silk Cut Blue ..."

"... her a light ..."

"... where you're sitting now ..."

"... one thing talking but ..."

"... a short with that ... ?"

"So what do we know about our suspect?"

Detective Kenny checks her notes and begins to rhyme off the facts. "John Crayn, DOB 1967, born and raised locally. Married his childhood sweetheart Olwyn Lavelle with whom he has two teenage children, Matthew and Emily. Self-employed as a tradesman, a plasterer; in the middle of the nineties began taking on contracts of his own and now has six other plasterers working for him. Made some money in the last few years when he successfully tendered for a couple of publicly funded projects—community centres, school extensions and a council housing development. But other than that, there is nothing to set him apart from any other man with a family in the area. He's well known and well liked, nothing else much to say about him."

"And he was seen in the company of Alice Rynne."

"Yes, we believe they met in his local. She was in the habit of going for a drink late at night before closing time. They were seen together laughing and flirting and we have word that he would sometimes drive her home at the end of the night. Because of that, people speculated that it developed into a relationship, which he denies."

"So she spends all day working on this thesis of hers and come nighttime she lays down her pen and goes for a drink."

"Something like that, it's only a seven-minute walk from the house to the village."

"Where she met this Crayn and struck up some sort of a relationship with him . . ."

"Which he denies."

"Was he in the pub on the night of Saturday twenty-sixth?"

"No and neither was she."

The detective shakes his head. "He may have been having an affair with her but that does not immediately give him a motive for killing her. What do we know about his wife, do we know anything about her?"

"We know they were childhood sweethearts, that they went to school together, and that they got married in their early twenties when she became pregnant. She works in a pharmaceutical firm; she went in as a production-line operative and gradually, by dint of hard work and study, rose to be head of HR. She has frequently been absent to the parent company in America for ongoing training."

"That's quite a rise, from production-line op. to head of the human resources division. How much focus and hard work do you need to achieve that?"

"Quite a lot, I'd imagine."

"I'd imagine your husband would be eating alone at home a lot of nights."

The detective considered. She has noticed that when he does this he lays the tip of his thumb against the front of his teeth. She watches him do it now and lets the silence develop fully until he finally looks up. "So, she's a corporate high-flier and he's a plasterer. I wonder is there anything there, has that made the marriage lopsided in some way or other. Some more background research into her might not go astray."

Detective Kenny nods and turns out through the door.

"He has a point," the man on the sofa says as he drains his mug before setting it on the ground.

"Does he?"

"Yes, your suspicion of my affair with this woman pushes the motive onto you. I may or may not be having an affair with this woman but the motive for killing her is yours, not mine. So now we have to ask where were *you* on the afternoon of Sunday twenty-seventh?"

"That's easy to answer. I did what I always do on Sunday afternoons. I went for a long walk with Emily Ruane, my childhood friend; we walked for two hours along the secondary roads, up through the bog and along the beach. We spoke to a couple of people on the way, waved to a couple of passing cars and it was after half past four when I got home. Emily will testify to that, we have been doing it for years. We hardly ever miss a summer Sunday." She looks at him keenly. "Of course, you know all that or did you think this ass keeps itself firm and trim all on its own?"

The lapse into cheap sarcasm does not suit her but it still needles him. He needs a moment to ride the swell of temper that blooms through his chest. There is something dangerous in the air between them, now. Everything from here on is a risk. He moves to close out the game.

"So where do we go from here, a woman we both know is dead but both of us have alibis which put us in the clear."

"You mean mine puts me in the clear. As we have already established, yours is seriously open to question."

The man shakes his head. "It's bent at the edges, not discredited. It can't be discarded on the basis of your suspicions; this investigation is at a dead end."

"That's sloppy," she scorns, "we have to be able to do better than that."

"Not me, I'm knackered." He throws his head onto the back of the sofa and opens his mouth to a huge yawn. He knows well that conceding the game will aggravate her. Seeing things through to the end, finishing what you start—these are some of the values by which she has succeeded in her world; she will not be able to let this go so easily. The man rouses himself and points at the screen.

"Matter a damn anyway, they're bringing the boyo in for interrogation now, we'll see what he has to say for himself."

He is the only suspect in the investigation and he sits in the interview room across the table from the detective. It is not often a straightforward case of murder proves so difficult, yielding so little in the way of leads or other avenues of investigation. All alibis have checked out and a full search of the house has thrown up nothing in the way of fibres or prints or weapons. So a lot depends on the statement given by this man sitting opposite him. Preliminary questioning has confirmed what the investigation already knows— he is forty years old, married with two kids in their late teens and, barring a couple of speeding tickets, he has no convictions.

The man is sitting with his hands clamped together on the table, his bullish strength giving the impression that he is all shoulders. He looks wholly misplaced in the interview room. His woollen cap lies on the table—he has been pulled off a worksite in the middle of a job—and there are clear traces of cement on his jacket and trousers. His wish to be anywhere else but in this dim, windowless room is obvious. He has already denied having an affair with the dead woman, having stated reasonably that it is neither unusual nor a crime to have flirted with her or bought her drinks. He has amused the senior detective by appealing to a shared blokeishness—she was young and pretty, what's a man to do? Nor is he able to add anything to what they already know about Alice Rynne. His account of her squares with what is common knowledge, with what anyone might pick up over a few shared drinks. And as the interview proceeds he has come to realize how little they know, how clueless the investigation is. The whole thing is grounded in nothing more than a few local rumours, precisely the sort of tittle-tattle that makes up the social static of any small community. Beneath his anxiety there grows a solid sense that he can refute everything they throw at him, that they have nothing to hold him on.

"I have nothing more to say," he says. "And by the looks of it, you have nothing, either."

The only revealing moment comes when the subject of his relationship with his wife is brought up. Is he happy in his marriage? He becomes defensive, laughing as if the question is utterly meaningless. The detective spots a chink and, by way of prising it open, he finds himself volunteering something about his own life.

"I'm happily married myself," he says blandly. "The best decision I ever made. Twelve years now and I cannot wait to clock off every evening. Come five o'clock I'm out of here before the fifth bell has sounded. And that myth about the obsessive cop who takes his work home with him . . ." The detective shakes his head and laughs, "Not me. My work stays here at my desk, dead woman or no dead woman. I go home, switch off the phone and play with my kids."

As he speaks, the detective finds himself becoming fond of his story, falling for it in a way he would not have wished. What exactly his motives were in revealing all this he cannot rightly say; what sort of empathic mood he hoped might develop between them he is not sure. Either way, the man opposite is having none of it. He shrugs his shoulders as if this has nothing to do with him and the detective knows that the interview is lost. It was a mistake bringing him in with so little to press him on. The interview stumbles on another half-hour through summary and repetition, summary and repetition, the drag of fatigue entering the room. In the middle of the afternoon the detective leaves and, shortly after, the duty officer comes in and tells the man that he is free to go. The man's surprise is genuine. He rises cautiously from the chair, glancing around him as if he expects someone in the room to administer a blow or a barked warning to sit back down—an interrogator's trick to scramble his defences and catch him off guard. But there is no one else in the room. To anyone watching, his anxious caution as he pulls the door behind him might confirm his innocence.

Later that evening the detective takes his turn in the pub, sitting at the end of the bar. He listens to the conversation among the other customers.

". . . shortly after the bit of grub in the afternoon . . ."

". . . up on scaffolding putting a scratch coat on the gable . . ."

"... two of them, suits and all ..."

"... a woman ..."

" ... pair of shoes on her ..."

"... washed his hawk and trowel ..."

"... no ..."

"... so I believe ..."

"... left on the mixer ..."

"... wouldn't be long ..."

"... quietened the cunt ..."

"... the same Johnny ..."

"... in fairness, though ..."

"... trousers covered in cement ..."

"... the shoes ruined ..."

"... last thing you'd be worried about ..."

"... thing on your mind ..."

"... lads up on the roof ..."

"... down from Christ what was happening ..."

"... looking at the whole thing ..."

"... the mixer still running ..."

It has been a disappointing episode, slow and irresolute and with none of the plot dynamics that have made the best episodes of the series such compulsive viewing. No reversals or recognitions, no antiphonal subplots. The episode has spent itself in a single storyline and made up the plot deficit by emphasizing the change to a village locale and the introduction of a new character. It is difficult to say at this early stage whether Detective Kenny will be a permanent feature. But she looks promising. She has been given a lot of screen time and there has been more than enough substance in the weighted exchanges between herself and her senior partner to suggest that she is here to stay. However, it appears that her first investigation is going to end in failure. The closing scene finds her standing in the afternoon sun, watching the suspect walk away across the car park. Her disappointment is obvious. The detective comes up behind her and steps up to his role as mentor and philosopher.

"So, what do you think?" she asks.

"I think he is as guilty as sin."

"And he walks away like this?"

"That's what the evidence allows."

"I thought we had him."

"Don't colour an investigation with faith or hope, Detective."

She grapples with this for a moment and then stores it away for further examination.

The suspect walks straight toward the camera, the sun full in his face. His features are set in a blank expression that does not falter as he settles the woollen cap on his head and continues walking until he blacks out the screen with the full of his chest. Cue the credits.

"For Christ's sake," the woman groans. "This programme gets worse and worse." She subsides heavily against the back of the sofa in exasperation.

"You heard the man—he's as guilty as sin."

"He gets to walk away, that's not good enough."

"We are given to believe that in some other world he will be brought to account in some other reckoning."

"Are we? I didn't see that. All I saw was him walking away scot-free."

He is not surprised to see her so frustrated but he is surprised that her disappointment is never tempered by the recurrence of such things. She has been critical of this series in the recent past, despairing of how it has fallen away from the character-driven plots of the early episodes. She has prophesied that it will not run for another season and yet still she is disappointed with it. And her sulk is genuine, a sullen mire with nothing girlish or alluring to it; a relentless hum of anger comes off her. He shifts himself into a sitting position.

"So," he says, "the O.J. scenario: if I did it, how and why?"

If she is grateful for the offer she does not show it. She takes it slow, giving deliberate vent to her rage. "It was like everything else in your life, a panicked reaction, an act of cowardice. Exactly the sort of bluster you could expect from someone who has never given life any serious thought."

There is everything of the pale accuser about her, now. He half-expects her to raise a finger to him and start ranting, driven by some terrible knowledge. But she seems to feel she has said enough, that nothing more is needed by way of explanation. He holds the silence and the long moment stretches between them. Eventually, he concedes with a sigh. He may as well, or they will be here to all hours.

"It's only a game," he says, "let's call it a night."

The look on her face has deepened beyond frustration to the expression of deep disgust. "I hate games," she whispers fervently. "Such a waste."

She will not be easily soothed from her frustration but he has no wish that she should go to bed in this mood.

He sits back and closes his eyes. "Okay, how did I do it?"

She shifts her weight to the edge of the sofa. "The detective is right, you struck her from behind with your left hand, one single blow—there was no sign of a struggle. Angles and blood spatter show that it had to be left-handed. There is no room for a right-handed person to swing against the wall." She swings her left hand in a wide arc to demonstrate. He shakes his head.

"Correction." He draws his right hand across his body to strike the same arc, backhanded. She shakes her head.

"Same angle of impact, yes, but you would never get enough force into it to do the job like that."

"Okay, so that's how I did it, but why?"

"It looks like a crime of passion but that's not what it was. It got out of hand as these things usually do. For you it was a couple of months' thoughtless fucking but for her it snagged her heart. All of a sudden she begins to have feelings for you. Look at her, her looks, look at her work—attachment disorders in Romanian adoptees—she is a passionate woman, the type of woman who will always be prey to her heart, always susceptible to its moods and qualms. And now she has these feelings and she cannot let you go. Also, there's this developed sense of melodrama—she has the panicked feeling that this might be her only chance at happiness. She cannot let this slip. So she starts making demands; she wants you to go away with her, leave your wife and kids, start anew. At first you fend her off with the usual excuses but by the end of three months she is frustrated. And then she threatens that she will go to your wife and tell all; that is the moment when things come to a head. You can't have that but you don't have the wit to argue your way out of it."

"So he whacks her?"

"You whack her. It looks like a crime of passion, the beautiful woman on the floor done in with a single blow to the head, but it is not like that. In fact, it is more an act of cowardice than anything else, the panicked response of someone who has never made a proper commitment to anything in his life."

You could be struck blind at this time of night, the man thinks. Not by what you see but by what you know others see; a kind of referred blindness. Because now he knows what she sees, looking at him down the years, down the length of this sofa. Her vantage point is that of a woman who has picked up a career and two languages while dropping a dress size and raising a family; from that standpoint anyone might see clearly. But she is not anyone, she is this woman, his wife, and he cannot think of a time when he did not fear her slightly. And now he knows why. You would not need to stand long in her shoes to see what she sees, to know the things she knows. The wonder is that he has not been blinded long ago.

She rises from the sofa and stands over him. She opens her mouth to say something but stops. And it's as if this moment has been waiting for them, waiting to be fulfilled as one instance of clear understanding between them. And so it is, and anything either of them might say now would be redundant, entirely beside the point. The moment wanes and she exits the room, pulling the door quietly behind her.

He remains on the sofa with his gaze fixed in the depths of the television screen.

He wakes early the following morning and sits up fully clothed on the sofa. After a moment, he stands up with a grimace and braces his hand in the small of his back before walking stiffly to the kitchen. There is milk in the fridge and he drinks it straight from the carton, wiping his mouth with the back of his hand. He pulls on his work boots and jacket before stepping outside.

The watch on his wrist tells him that it's not yet half-seven and at this early hour the sky looks contused, frayed. It has rained during the night and the grass and hedges look especially vivid, pressing toward him out of the grey light. He pats himself down, jacket and trouser, checking for fags, phone, keys—all the things he will need for the day ahead. As he stands there frisking himself, the discussion of the night before comes back to him and it is as vivid as if he had just walked away from it, as if a whole night's sleep had never intervened. Once again he is in the grip of that cold anxiety. He should have known better than to go head to head with her in something like that; he was never a match for her. But he was shocked at the lengths to which she was prepared to go, the damage she risked; he had never seen her so reckless and wilful before.

At this early hour, the light falls at a low angle across the fields, running ahead of itself, drawing shadows in its wake. This is the time of day when search teams fan out across open ground looking for those shallow troughs in which shadows pool, those elongated depressions that turn out to be shallow graves into which the earth has slumped over abdominal and thoracic collapse, over what remains of the heart . . . And standing there, he wonders how he knows such stuff. Did he read it or see it, who could have told him? It seems a strange topic to dwell on at this hour of the day—or any hour, for that matter. And there is something shameful about knowing such a thing. He suspects that it takes a peculiar hollowness to know it, to be bothered by it at all; an inner, ringing emptiness in which such knowledge might come to rest.

Of course the real question is not how he knows such stuff but whether it is worth knowing at all and at what price does knowing it come. Was something crucial displaced within him when he learned this, something meaningful and essential, something to do with the real, congested stuff of a lived life? It seems obvious that there should be more pressing worries than this to occupy his mind . . . He stands there a while, lost in these thoughts. Then, after a second frisk he finds his keys and moves around the gable of the house toward his van.

A man can only know so much, he thinks. Or more accurately, there is only so much a man needs to know.

Prophet X

So I told Leo that I'd finally got to meet Halloran.

This piece of news flew over Leo's head because just then he started to talk about something else entirely and past experience has told me that there's no point cutting across him when he's in full spate. Better to let him continue and talk things out. Besides, I was interested to see that Leo was more than a little confused as to what he was talking about himself.

"So," he says, "she takes my hand and places it inside her shirt and sure enough I feel this cable, like a short length of flex in her breast. I never felt anything like it. Apparently some gizmo fitted in her chest so that whenever her heartbeat falls below a certain rate this thing kicks in with a couple of hundred volts to kick-start her. What do you think of that?"

"I sympathize."

"I don't want sympathy—I'd prefer if you had some ideas."

"It's some sort of a pacemaker."

"No, it's more sudden and aggressive than that."

"Well then, I don't know. But you're after telling me that the last two women you touched were crossed with metal. Am I right?"

"Yes, one with this resuscitative gizmo in her chest, a Czech waitress, and the other with a line of countersunk screws holding a metal plate in her head."

"I don't know whether to laugh or to cry. The fault might be yours."

"My fault?"

"Yes."

"How my fault?"

"Maybe it's a case of you laying your hands on these women and that's what happens to them—that's the effect you have on them—all of a sudden they turn to metal."

Leo grimaced with disappointment. "Even if the idea had some merit it doesn't take into account the fact that in each case these women took my hand and laid it on themselves. It wasn't a case of me going up and pawing them."

"Okay, you're absolved of all blame. I admit that makes things more complex."

"All I'm saying is that there's something odd out there, something funny happening. I read somewhere the other day that ten percent of American citizens meet the definition of a cyborg."

The redundancy of the statement is obvious. I cannot resist the temptation to speak slowly and deliberately, like I'm correcting a child.

"This isn't America, Leo."

"I know well it's not America but I will tell you what it is. This is the city with the youngest demographic in the whole country and yet there is more money spent here per head of population on cosmetic surgery than anywhere else. Did you know that?"

As it happens, I did know that. A couple of days ago I had

watched a breakfast TV show that ran a feature on the absence of oversight and regulation in the cosmetic surgery industry. And sure enough, I too was amazed to hear some survey cited, which showed that there was more money spent in this city on implants and augmentation than anywhere else in the country.

"And," Leo continued, "forty percent of all surgery carried out in European hospitals has nothing to do with being curative or alleviating pain; forty percent and rising." His tone is that of someone clinching a decisive point. "It's an escalating pattern, something cumulative. God knows what it all means."

I have no idea what he is driving at, so I nod my head and keep quiet. Sometimes it's just better to let Leo speak. I'd rung him earlier in the day to meet up for a pint because there was something about this Halloran thing that bothered me and I wanted to run it by him. Leo is a man of ideas and if there is something I'm not seeing or missing then he is the one to spot it.

In the early afternoon, the pub is quiet. There's a man at the counter reading the paper and over at the window a couple of tourists. A young woman is setting beer mats on the tables by the wall.

"So you finally managed to track Halloran down," Leo says suddenly.

"Yes," I said, "finally."

"And you were granted an audience?"

"Yes."

"Where was he holed up?"

Halloran was sitting in a blaze of winter sunshine when I met him. Three weeks of phone calls and texts and postponements had finally led me to the third floor of a new office building on the docks—one of those new developments that still had the builder's signage on the front and TO LET posters in the lower windows. Halloran's corner office was a raw concrete and glass affair with the sockets and conduit still naked in the walls. He was sitting with his back to the window, which overlooked the docks, a silver glare shining off the sea that stretched away under the low sun.

"I can only offer a chair," he called as I entered.

"A chair is fine."

"What is the most severe global shortage?"

The question caught me on the hop. A moment's frantic scrabbling around in my head followed but I did not think my answer was too shabby.

"Potable water," I said, "literacy."

"Wrong," he called loudly, even though there was less than eight feet between us. "The most severe shortage in the world, the direst shortage, is of hope—all those other things—water and literacy—are subsequent to having some place we can put our hopes, something we can get out of bed for and live our life toward."

"And this is where Cosan comes in."

"Yes, the world has faith in nature but its hope is in technology. And hope is what we're dealing in."

"Cosan's the name of this new technology?" Leo interjected.

"No, Cosan's the name of the company it's registered to. It's from an old Irish word that means 'path' or 'way.' Anyway, this company specializes in digital security; it has several patents to its name."

"And this Halloran is the head honcho?"

"Yes, he's managing director, head of research, majority stakeholder, the whole lot."

"He's the kiddie."

"Yes, he's the kiddie, the daddy. All those titles are a bit grandiose—we're talking about a small company with around six people in it. But yes, Halloran is the man."

"Paint a picture for me, an image to work with."

"Mid-forties I'd say, shoulder-length hair and oversize shirt with a grey suit. Hard to tell if this was the natural appearance of a man who didn't care how he looked or if it was all a careful piece of corporate, bohemian schtick. In so far as it had me wondering, it was very effective. And a ringing voice, booming away, exactly what you'd expect from a man who had thrown down a challenge to the world."

"A middle-aged X-er?"

"I suppose, I never gave it that much thought."

"And this is the fella who put the famous advert in *The Economist*—how did he account for that?"

"It was a real attention-grabber, wasn't it?" Halloran said with a grin. "The scientific community was ablaze with our name within an hour of that issue going online. But you have to understand the magnitude of our claim: a small company out of nowhere claiming to have invented a system which produces clean, renewable energy; a company which claims to have subverted the second law of thermodynamics."

Halloran threw up his arms in a hieratic gesture. "If you are making such a claim you need to make it loud and proud—so where better than the bible of the corporate world? It got people's attention, alright."

"Yes, it did," I conceded. "But I've looked up all those online threads and forums, and the majority of contributors were, to put it mildly, sceptical. Most were immediately hostile to your claim."

"So they were, as we had anticipated they would be. But go back to the advert again—it wasn't just making a revolutionary claim, it was also an invitation for scientists to step forward and validate our claim; we called for a panel of experts. And it worked in spades. We were deluged with CVs from all over the world—corporate and government-funded labs, universities and research institutes—Bell Labs, the Max Planck Institute, MIT, BNFL, Sony Industries—a *Who's Who* of research facilities despatching their best brains to examine our claim. And, of course, we also had loads of interest from the energy sector— Exxon and Shell and BP, they wanted to come to the party, too. Within a week we had over three hundred CVs from all over the globe. Every one of them might have thought we were shysters but they still wanted to see for themselves. That advert was eighty grand well spent."

Leo nodded. "Eighty grand in the right place buys a lot of cred and authority. And he's targeting a very specific audience when he puts it in *The Economist*. Presumably that's why he chose a business magazine and not a scientific journal."

"Exactly," Halloran said. "We make no bones about this technology being a commercial proposition, and our need for investment capital. So the ad was placed to draw the attention of potential investors as well as the scientific community."

"And it worked?"

"Oh yes." He swung his arm around at the bare concrete walls. "Looking at this you might not think so, but we are in negotiations with several potential investors."

I turned a new page of my notebook. Clean paper emerging with each turn always went some distance toward clearing my mind. And I needed all my wits about me in this room.

"Just to backtrack a moment," I said. "Let's try to be clear on the magnitude of your claim. From what I know, this technical challenge has defeated the greatest minds since the dawn of civilization—Archimedes, Galileo, da Vinci, Edison—all these geniuses have squared up to this challenge and every one of them has come away defeated. Ten years ago the American patents office issued an advisory that they would not entertain anyone claiming to have such an invention . . ."

"...and now a small company with no history in this sort of technology starts jumping up and down and shouting, 'Over here, over here,' and claiming to have this invention which will prove to be nothing less than epoch-making—that's what you're thinking?" Halloran beckoned the question with open hands.

"It's what the whole scientific community is thinking. Your claim is to deny the second law of thermodynamics; it could hardly be more radical or extravagant."

"Yes, that is the epochal magnitude of this invention; there is no point in being diffident about it. When this technology is rolled out we can honestly talk of the world making a new start, it will be the beginning of a new era, a new history, a new calendar. At one stroke this will set aside all environmental worries, it will bridge the poverty gap—it will put cheap, limitless energy in the hands of the poorest countries, it will ..."

Leo guffawed. "That sermon must have sounded odd in light of the public failure of the demo."

"That speech would sound odd in any context."

The demo was scheduled as a live stream from the Kinetica Museum in London. When I logged on that Friday afternoon, the camera angle showed a glass cube on a plinth containing a stationary, plastic disc on a small spindle fixed between two supporting brackets. Behind the display cube a large window showed the traffic passing in a wet blur of metal and glass. A scrolling notice on the screen informed that the demonstration had been postponed due to technical reasons. I sat for a long while watching the forlorn stillness of the glass cube and I could not help thinking that it looked like the home of a domestic pet that had just died. After a few minutes, a bulky shadow drifted into shot and I watched as a cleaner swung a mop over the floor, back and forth, moving heedlessly across the screen.

Leo leaned onto the table with both elbows. "Since there was no demo, I guess it technically could not be classed a failure."

"That's Halloran's point, too. Seemingly they hadn't factored in the heat from the overhead lighting rig which was used to illumine the live stream. They claimed that it warped some of the components on the prototype so the demo couldn't run."

"I've never heard of the Kinetica Museum."

"I had to look it up myself—it's in London, near Spitalfields, and it's a respected avant-garde gallery specializing in work which combines art and technology."

"Sounds like an unusual place to have a commercial demo."

"Yes, it is unusual. As a rule, new technologies are demonstrated to invited audiences of industry heads and so on, likely investors. I can't think of another instance where a new commercial technology was demoed like this."

The barman left two pints on the table between us and I counted out the exact change. Leo gazed blankly at the pints and then settled back in the chair.

"Suppose we take Halloran at his word for the moment, what sort of plans does he have for this technology? What sort of systems does he hope to deploy it in?"

Halloran shook his head. "Cosan doesn't see itself being involved in the production side of things. Our plan is to license it out to developers who will configure it however they want. It is fully scaleable, up or down; it can be used to drive MP3 players or power entire cities. But Cosan does not see itself involved in that end of it—we see ourselves as more research oriented."

"Halloran is really convincing on this kind of detail—he has all the ready answers and the whole scenario mapped out in his mind. And he's not embarrassed to talk up this thing as if it were the salvation of the world. But, what's really interesting is to hear the language he uses when he talks about it. It's almost evangelical—he speaks of hope and faith—'We have faith in nature but we put our hope in technology'—that's a mantra he repeated a couple of times. And there was this really surreal moment when he seemed to drift from the topic altogether and started riffing about something else entirely."

Halloran fell silent and lowered his chin onto his chest. The gesture was so completely off-hand, so devoid of any connection to what we had been talking about, that I knew for certain he had forgotten all about me. For a long moment his self-absorption was so complete I did not dare rouse him. Behind him the afternoon light deepened over the sea. Eventually, Halloran drew his hand across his face and resumed in a sombre tone.

"This is all very public and that's exactly the way I want it. I can take all the scepticism and the ridicule; I can handle all that. My biggest fear is that one morning I will come into our lab and find the whole thing smashed up, all our prototypes destroyed, all our software scrambled. That's what I'm afraid of."

"So you're hiding in plain sight."

"Not hiding, just hoping that being out in the open safeguards me and my work from disappearing in the middle of the night into some fucking unmarked facility without any redress."

"Some might say that's a bit paranoid."

Halloran guffawed in derision. 'Do your research, for Christ's sake. Do you have any idea how this technology cuts across the interests of some very powerful industries? Have you thought of the military applications? Do you know what they are capable of doing?" And on that rhetorical question he drifted away once more, carried off on this sudden gust of anger.

"When I heard that, I just sat there and said nothing, I couldn't believe that his delusion ran that deep."

Leo shook his head. "In fairness, no one has disproved his claim yet so no one can rightly say that he is delusional. As far as I can make out, there are three options: he is either the real thing or a knowing fraud or . . ."

". . . an honest eejit. Yes, I know."

"So what's your read on him?"

"Oh, he's a true believer. Once you get beyond all the bluster and the self-dramatizing you come up against a man who has complete faith in what he's talking about."

"So his delusion is all the more complete."

"Maybe he really has hit on something."

"If he has, and it is what he says it is, then we're talking about another Copernicus—something that big."

"I agree and so would he. From what I gathered, that's the epoch-making dimension to which this man thinks he's playing. Nothing less than a complete historical break."

Leo leans onto the table and clasps both hands together. There is a brightness about him that I have not seen in the longest time. And this kind of attentiveness is a bonus, something well beyond what I had expected. The most I had hoped for was that he might furrow his brow, and voice a couple of sharp observations against which I would clarify my own thoughts. I am heartened to find him so completely taken up with the story. As he looks up I blurt out, "And he uses a strange phrase when he speaks of selling this technology—he speaks of trying 'to persuade people to our proposition.' That's the language of an ideologue."

Leo's face is fully open now, sharp with sudden energy. "Backtrack a second, what did you say the name of the company was?"

"Cosan."

Leo's fingers are hopping on the table. Recently he's talked about giving up the fags; I wonder if he's managed it.

"And what about the validation process?"

"The advert in *The Economist* called for physicists and engineers to submit CVs and résumés. It made a commitment to put together a panel of experts who would examine the technology and go public with their findings."

"And they're still working on it."

"So I gather."

Leo runs his hand through his hair and lowers his gaze to the table. He stays like this a long time and when he finally looks up I am anxious to see that he is having trouble keeping a straight face.

"How long have you been working on this story?"

"Off and on for three months. To tell the truth, I'm tired of the whole thing but I just can't seem to let it go. I don't even know if there is a story in it any more."

Leo's face opens over his teeth in a wide, unhealthy smile. "Oh, there's a story alright," he grins, "but maybe it's not the one you think. Three months and you haven't put it together?"

"Put what together?"

"The evidence, the clues, the whole fucking thing."

I shake my head. A heave of anxiety passes through me; something in me will not survive the next few minutes. Leo is dismayed. Now his tone is deliberate, slowly instructive.

"Start with the name—Cosan—a word which has its origins in the Irish word for 'path' or 'way.' And this Cosan comes up with a technology which is bruited as epoch-making, nothing less than the salvation of the earth, in fact. And furthermore, this machine is validated by a jury of good men and true—let me guess, twelve in number?"

"Yes."

"Of course. Now does any of this not sound familiar or do I have to drag a child in off the street to spell it out for you?"

The blurred outline is indeed visible but I refuse to draw the whole thing together into a coherent picture. Too mad, too unbelievable. Leo sees me struggling.

"For Christ's sake, can you not see what this is all about?"

"I see it but I can't believe it."

"Look at the evidence," Leo persists, "the separate parts of it—the name, the epochal nature of this technology, its mission of salvation, the twelve men who attest to its miraculous powers . . . okay, they're not fishermen or tax collectors, but engineers and scientists will do just as well to spread the word. And he spoke of it in terms of faith and hope, didn't he?"

"Yes, several times."

"He's straying into complex territory here—two of the theological virtues, the ones freely given by God's grace. I'll bet he didn't speak much of the third one—charity."

"No, not that I remember."

"I doubt if he did, it would present special difficulties to an entrepreneur. I'll tell you how this is going to end. My bet is that there are plans to eventually float this whole thing on the stock exchange, possibly with an initial share price set within reach of the private investor, a people's price. I believe the word is . . ."

". . . incorporated, yes, I see it now."

"Cosan Inc. or Christ Inc., whichever you prefer. Either way, it's destined to be the world leader in Christ machines or redemption technologies."

Leo sits back, his face open in pure wonder. He is transported, wholly in thrall to the idea. In the gloom of the pub his eyes glitter with delight. I am thinking again of Halloran and that farcical interview. His pale face is clear to me, vivid as he riffed away on the possibility of threats to his work and personal safety. Now the abduction scenario, with all its laboured hints of maltreatment and disappearance, has a different sense to it.

As a paranoid fantasy it is prosaic; as a dream of crucifixion it is not unsubtle.

"Did you hear that?" Leo points toward the ceiling.

"What?"

"Listen."

The news headlines are on and they are not good. They wash through the pub in a grey wave. Stock markets across Europe continue to fall in the wake of a huge American investment bank filing for bankruptcy; the ECB has issued a bleak warning on interest rates, and at home, the government denies there is any liquidity problem in our banking system. Leo turns to me and spreads his hands.

"This is what I am talking about—a gathering chaos, something so deep and widespread it can only be resolved by divine intervention. And this is Halloran and his technology, the *Deus ex Machina*, the god from the machine; *techne* and *logos* finally brought together. And of course it's only right and fitting that Christ should come by way of the machine this time. He tried the flesh and blood route before—it ended badly, as I remember."

The waitress passes behind Leo. She is carrying a large mug of coffee and a pint toward the couple sitting inside the window. I watch as she rises onto her toes, turning her hips to pass in the narrow space between the tables. As she raises her arms her T-shirt lifts up out of her jeans, exposing the lower part of her back. She is tanned, her skin like brushed gold. And right at the base of her spine, precisely where I imagine her whole nervous system converges, I see that she carries a mark. I get the merest glimpse of it, but even as it passes in a rhythmic blur it's unmistakeable—a bar-code tattoo complete with a row of digits beneath. She moves on toward the couple at the window where she is lit by sunlight pouring in from the street. Leo sees nothing of this. Lost in his own thoughts, he sweeps a hand through the air.

"Electric women and redemption machines: the world is ripe for a miracle. All that's needed now are men of good faith, true believers. Men like me and you, Jimmy, me and you."

It's been a long time since I've seen Leo this happy.

And I'd forgotten just how uneasy that makes me.